Meet the Rookie K-9 Unit officers and their brave police dog partners

Officer: Zoe Trent

Age: 27

K-9 Partner: Freya the Belgian Tervuren

Assignment: Protect her old friend Sean Murphy and his disabled son from the danger that is stalking them.

Officer: Dalton West

Age: 33

K-9 Partner: Luna the brindle mutt

Assignment: Protect Josie Callahan and her daycare center from the criminals who are targeting it.

Valerie Hansen was thirty when she awoke to the presence of the Lord in her life and turned to Jesus. She now lives in a renovated farmhouse in the breathtakingly beautiful Ozark Mountains of Arkansas and is privileged to share her personal faith by telling the stories of her heart for Love Inspired. Life doesn't get much better than that!

Lenora Worth writes award-winning romance and romantic suspense. Three of her books finaled in the ACFW Carol Awards, and her Love Inspired Suspense novel *Body of Evidence* became a *New York Times* bestseller. Her novella in *Mistletoe Kisses* made her a *USA TODAY* bestselling author. With sixty books published and millions in print, she goes on adventures with her retired husband, Don, and enjoys reading, baking and shopping...especially shoe shopping. Visit her on the web at lenoraworth.com.

ROOKIE
K-9 UNIT
CHRISTMAS

VALERIE HANSEN
LENORA WORTH

HARLEQUIN® LOVE INSPIRED® SUSPENSE

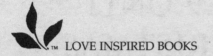

LOVE INSPIRED BOOKS

Recycling programs
for this product may
not exist in your area.

ISBN-13: 978-0-373-67791-7

Rookie K-9 Unit Christmas

Copyright © 2016 by Harlequin Books S.A.

Thanks and acknowledgment are given to Valerie Hansen
and Lenora Worth for their participation in the Rookie K-9 Unit series.

Surviving Christmas
Copyright © 2016 by Harlequin Books S.A.

Holiday High Alert
Copyright © 2016 by Harlequin Books S.A.

www.Harlequin.com

Printed in U.S.A.

CONTENTS

SURVIVING CHRISTMAS

Valerie Hansen

Many thanks to Lenora Worth for her friendship and expert advice as we put these two novellas together.

And continuing love to my Joe, who is with me in spirit, looking over my shoulder and offering moral support as I write. He always will be.

For He shall give His angels charge over thee,
to keep thee in all thy ways.
–*Psalms* 91:11

ONE

Sean Murphy hated to close his eyes. A terrifying past waited for him in sleep, a past that sometimes invaded even his waking hours. Love for his six-year-old son, Patrick, was what kept him sane, kept him battling to return to normal. Patrick needed him, now more than ever. All they had left was each other.

The St. Louis apartment Sean had rented on his return to the States was small but adequate for the present. The future would take care of itself. At least Sean hoped so. There had been a time when he'd believed God was guiding him through life. Now, he felt adrift.

Fog of sleep dulled his senses, but not so much that he failed to hear a strange sound in the dark. He froze. Listened intently. Heard nothing more. Sighing, he wished he knew how to stop being so jumpy. Every creak of the old building brought irrational fear.

A cadence of soft steps followed. Sean sat bolt upright. "Patrick?"

The sound ceased. Sean slipped out of bed, wishing he still had his rifle and full battle gear. St. Louis might not be Kandahar, but that didn't mean there was no danger. Yes, his emotions were raw. And, yes, chances were that he was merely imagining a threat. There was only one way to find out. He must see for himself.

Since Patrick's near-drowning accident in the swimming pool at his maternal grandparents' estate, the boy had been having trouble with speech as well as motor skills. Therefore, he sometimes sought out his daddy without explanation. That was probably what Sean had heard. Still, he refused to disregard an instinctive warning.

Barefoot, he tiptoed to the open bedroom door and waited in the shadow from the night-light in the hallway. A low mumble reached him. How could Patrick be talking in his sleep when he had so much trouble doing so awake?

Sean pressed his back to the jamb and slowly eased forward. The voices were clear. For an instant he wished they weren't.

"I ain't killin' no kid. You got that?" one person grumbled.

"We aren't supposed to. Just the father."

"Fine. What if the kid sees us? What then?"

"Nobody'll know we're here if you shut your yap," the other prowler whispered. "Come on."

Sean tensed. He was strong, ready to defend himself, but anything might happen if Patrick awoke. The boy's most frequent utterance was a high-pitched squeal of fright and frustration. If he began to carry on like that, the attackers might change their minds and harm him, too.

Going on the offense was the answer. Sean grabbed the junior baseball bat he'd bought to help Patrick regain coordination and braced himself.

The first man led with his pistol, giving Sean a one-time chance of disarming him. Wood in the child's bat cracked as Sean brought it down on the assailant's wrist. The man dropped the gun, doubled up and howled. His partner didn't wait for him to recover. Instead, he fired blindly in the dark, then turned tail and ran.

Sean dove for the gun and connected. Its owner leaped onto his back and tried to wrest it away. He might have succeeded if he'd had both hands in working order—or if his cohort had stuck around to help.

Sean continued to struggle with the man in the confines of the narrow hallway. His temple hit a doorjamb. Flashes of light, like exploding mortar shells, blinded him. Noises of war filled his ears. The acrid smell of gunpowder and the portent of death seemed to be everywhere.

A trickle of blood wet his close-cropped hair as survival instinct locked his fingers around the cold metal in his hands. At that moment, nothing could have pried open his grip.

There was a muted crash, then a tinkling, rustling sound. Clarity returned enough to suggest that the first man had stumbled over the Christmas tree he and Patrick had just decorated.

A child screamed.

Patrick!

Lunging, Sean knocked the intruder aside and struggled to his feet, gun in hand. That was enough. The injured man scrambled away, rounded the corner into the living room and disappeared out the door.

Sean wanted to follow. To capture at least one of the thugs who had declared their intent to kill him. But he didn't. Patrick needed him more. The child came first. Always had. Always would.

So, now what?

Police officer Zoe Trent had recently graduated from Canyon County K-9 Training Center in Desert Valley, Arizona, with her Belgian Tervuren, Freya. Being partnered with a specialized K-9 had been a goal of hers ever since completing the police academy. Now that it was time to return to her regular assignment in Mesa, Arizona, however, she knew she was going to miss the new friends she'd made during the twelve-week K-9 training program.

Wishing there were an easy way to keep in touch, and knowing they would surely drift apart as normal life resumed, she'd struggled to fall asleep tonight. A Christmas carol ringtone on her cell phone startled her awake.

Freya barked to accompany her muttered, "Hello?"

"Zoe?"

"Yes." Coming alert, she raised on one elbow.

"It's me again. Sean Murphy. Sorry to bother you, but you did tell me to call if I needed anything."

Instant worry for her college chum infused her. "Of course. What's wrong? You sound awful. Have you had another PTSD flashback?"

"It's worse than that."

Her dark eyes narrowed, and she raked stray tendrils of long brown hair away from her face with her free hand. "How can it be worse? It's not Patrick again, is it?"

"He's okay, so far. There's nobody here I can trust, and I really need help. Somebody's trying to kill me."

"What?" How could she express doubt without jeopardizing their seasoned friendship? "Are you sure? I mean, you told me you'd been a little confused since your medical discharge."

"I know what you're thinking," he countered. "I had the same misgivings. I've been awake for hours since this happened, trying to figure it out. Two guys broke into my apartment, and I fought with one of them."

"Did you call the police?"

"Of course. You know how it is in a big city. If the prowlers had succeeded in shooting me, I'd have gotten more attention."

"The men were armed?"

"Yes. One is now sporting a broken wrist, I hope. I disarmed him and he ran. So did his partner."

Zoe paused to choose her words carefully. "Okay. You had a break-in. What makes you think these guys had murder on their minds?"

"I heard them say they were there to kill me." He hesitated, then added, "I know I wasn't hallucinating because of what happened next. When I hit one on his gun hand, the other fired and left a bullet in the ceiling. The cops took all the evidence. Since nothing was stolen and nobody got shot, they acted like they didn't hold out much hope to catch the guys."

"Unless the ballistics match another case," she said. "Do you think these assailants might have been old friends of Sandra's?" Zoe hated to bring up his late wife but felt compelled to ask. After all, the woman had overdosed while her innocent son was floundering in the deep end of a swimming pool.

"I can't see why drug dealers would have it in for me," Sean said. "Their business was with Sandra."

"Agreed. So, how can I help you?"

"You can get me into that service dog program you mentioned when I was first discharged. I need to get my emotions under better control if I intend to survive more real life attacks."

"Okay. I'll see the director, Ellen Foxcroft, and put your name on her waiting list."

"That's not enough. Not after last night."

Zoe could tell from his tone that he was approaching an emotional crossroad and wished they were face-to-face so she could judge his condition more accurately. "Are you and Patrick out of danger now?"

"Temporarily. I threw some clothes and stuff into the pickup, and I've been driving around, thinking, ever since the police left. I can't take him back to the apartment. Whoever came after me last night may try again."

"What about going to your in-laws? They have plenty of room for both of you, don't they?"

"I'd rather hole up in a cardboard box on the street than rely on them," Sean said. "The Shepherds were so concerned with excusing Sandra's addiction and transferring blame, they laid it all on me."

"Okay. Tell you what," Zoe said, hoping her

growing concern was masked, "why don't you come on down to Desert Valley to visit me? I was going to head back to Mesa soon, but there's no hurry. I don't start my new assignment until after the first of the year, and the Desert Valley PD can use a few substitute cops here while their regulars take holiday time off."

"What good will a few weeks do me?"

"It'll give you a chance to chill out, for one thing. Besides, once Ellen meets you and Patrick and realizes how special your needs are, maybe she'll make an exception and work you in."

The quiet on the other end of the line troubled her. The Sean Murphy she'd met in college was nothing like this traumatized widower. Coming home from combat with PTSD was bad enough without having to face the death of his spouse and near loss of his only child.

"All right," Sean finally said.

She almost cheered. Instead, she said, "I'm looking forward to it. And to meeting Patrick."

Silence again. Then, "He's not himself yet. He may never be. Doctors keep reminding me there are no guarantees."

"That doesn't matter."

Anger tinged his reply. "Of course it does."

"No," Zoe told him tenderly. "It doesn't. He's your son and you love him. That's enough for me."

Although Sean's goodbye was terse, she could tell he was touched by her total acceptance. She didn't have to see the boy to know he merited a good life with the parent who was willing to sacrifice anything to help him. Everyone deserved a fighting chance at happiness.

Even babies who are born with fatal birth defects, she added, blinking rapidly. She had not wept for her nameless baby brother since she was five years old and a stranger had come to take him away. Mama had cried then, but Daddy had stood dry-eyed, staring at the tiny, imperfect bundle wrapped in the blue blanket.

That was the last time Zoe had been permitted to talk about the absent baby. It was as if he had never been born, which was apparently exactly what her parents had wanted.

The sense of injustice and concern for the helpless had begun then and had built throughout her formative years, perhaps even directing her path into law enforcement. She didn't trust easily, but she did have a soft heart for the downtrodden.

Like Patrick. And like his daddy.

Sean's next stop was the bank, where he withdrew all but a few dollars of his savings via the drive-through window. If there was any chance he was being tracked or followed, cash would be a necessity.

And speaking of being followed…

A black SUV seemed to be dogging them. It was back several car lengths, yet changed lanes whenever he did. His hands tightened on the wheel. His little boy was strapped in, of course, but that didn't mean it would be safe to take evasive action, particularly if excessive speed was involved. Where were the cops when you needed them?

Sean whipped around a corner, determined to find a patrol car or police station. He checked his mirrors. The SUV was gone. Had he merely imagined it trailing them? *Imagined* was the key, wasn't it? His mind was good at seeing enemies around every corner and behind every door, the way they'd been in Afghanistan. His body had come home, but part of his mind was still over there, still caught up in the fighting.

He couldn't afford to show signs of instability. If the authorities concluded he was an unfit parent, they might take Patrick away. Worse, with no other close relatives available, they might place him with his negligent maternal grandparents.

The only thing that mattered to Sean was his own assurance that Patrick was absolutely safe with him. If he'd thought otherwise, he'd have stepped back and voluntarily relinquished custody.

Glancing in the rearview mirror at his curly haired look-alike strapped into the narrower backseat he smiled. "You getting hungry, buddy?"

Patrick nodded.

"How about a quick burger? You like those, don't you?"

Another nod.

"Sorry," Sean said, urging speech the way the therapist had. "I don't quite understand you. Can you say yes or no?"

The little boy looked back at his daddy with eyes as blue as the sky, smiled and said, "No."

"Did you just make a *joke*?" Sean's eyes misted.

Patrick's grin spread as he said, "Yes," and Sean was so excited by the possibility he almost let his pickup truck drift to the curb.

In moments, however, his pulse returned to normal. Patrick began to chant, "Yes, no, yes, no," as if neither word meant anything to him.

Monitoring the traffic behind him, Sean picked up some fast food, then headed for the highway that would take him southwest to Desert Valley. He might not have an abundance of friends willing to stand with him, but at least he had one.

He'd checked his side-and rearview mirrors repeatedly and had seen no sign of the SUV that had worried him before. Nevertheless, the sooner he reached Zoe Trent, the better.

"Sean's an old college friend who just got out of the army on a medical discharge," Zoe told lead K-9 unit trainer Sophie Williams. "I was hoping you could have a word with Ellen Foxcroft and see if she can work him in to the therapy dog program."

"And leave who else out?" Sophie was scowling.

Zoe knew her position as a rookie K-9 officer from Sophie's most recent graduating class gave her very little influence. Nevertheless, she had to keep trying. "Maybe, since I've offered to hang around DVPD until after the holidays and sub, I could volunteer my services to you in my downtime and we could squeeze in an extra student and dog. There's no place else I need to be, and I don't have to report to work with Freya until after the first of the year."

Looking for moral support, Zoe laid her hand on the Belgian Tervuren's head and scratched behind her silky, erect ears. Fellow students had teased her about being assigned to a dog whose fur almost matched her own dark brown hair. That was fine with her.

"All right. I'll speak to Ellen for you," Sophie said.

Zoe thought she'd better give Sophie a little more information about Sean, including that he and his son would be staying with her. She explained about the PTSD. "And he's a widower. His wife overdosed while she was supposed to be watching their son, Patrick. The boy survived almost drowning but was left with brain damage. It's a really sad story."

"Well, sounds like he has a good friend in you," Sophie said. "All right. As soon as your friend gets settled, bring him in for an interview. What do you intend to do with Sean's son while he's being assessed and maybe trained?"

"I thought I'd see if Marilyn and Josie would accept him in their day care. Patrick does have special needs, though."

Sophie nodded. "Lily likes it there, and Ryder and I are pleased with the facility. She's not my stepdaughter yet but it won't be long."

"Hey, if the police chief approves the place and so do you, I'm sure that'll put Sean at ease." Encouraged and uplifted by her trainer's support, Zoe laid a hand lightly on Sophie's arm. "Thanks. This means a lot to me."

"Don't thank me," Sophie said. "Nothing has happened yet."

"But it will, God willing," Zoe countered with a grin. "This is the perfect time of the year. Patrick can go to Sunday school and maybe even participate with other kids in the Christmas pageant."

"We can always use another shepherd or angel," Sophie said. "Lily and I are playing Magi. I'm working on camel costumes for Ryder's old dog Titus and another yellow Lab. Probably Tristan McKeller's Jesse." She paused. "Come to think of it, Tristan's a former soldier. Maybe he can offer your friend some advice."

Zoe stopped smiling and shook her head slowly, thoughtfully. Tristan, a Desert Valley police officer, was a good guy, but... "I don't know. Sean may not want to air his problems. It will all come out if and when he qualifies for the Canine Assistance program, of course, but since I didn't ask if I could tell anyone else, would you mind keeping the story to yourself?"

"Of course," Sophie said. "You did mention he had some kind of trouble in St. Louis, though. If it follows him here, I will need to share his story with Ryder."

"I understand. And thanks." Sighing, Zoe remembered her old friend Sean and his boyish good looks. She'd had a crush on him from the first moment she'd laid eyes on him, and when he'd proudly announced his plans to marry coed Sandra Shepherd, it had nearly broken her heart.

Hopefully whoever broke into his apartment doesn't figure out where he's gone, she thought, realizing she did believe his story of the attack. If thugs came after him here, their actions would certainly be taken seriously. The advantage she—and Sean—had while in Desert Valley was her close ties with the police department and the Canyon County K-9 Training Center.

Nobody was going to pull the wool over the eyes of the officials here, let alone fool trained dogs whose senses were so well honed.

The previous batch of rookies and their K-9 partners had helped nab a serial killer. If anyone should be scared of coming to Desert Valley, it should be criminals.

Zoe smiled. Strangers here stood out like bright

blossoms on a Cholla cactus in December. Nobody was going to bother Sean and his son. Not while she and her friends were on duty.

TWO

Despite the terrain in Desert Valley being anything but Christmas-like, Sean noticed red and green decorations hung from every light post, and twinkling lights festooned the fronts of businesses along the main street of the small Arizona town.

As he looked for a place to park, he glanced in the rearview mirror at Patrick, who was still fast asleep in his car seat, then pulled to the curb in front of the only official-looking building he saw. He let his truck idle while he called Zoe's cell. "I'm here. Where are you?"

"Already? What did you do, drive night and day?"

"As a matter of fact, yes. I'm in front of the police station. I'd planned to go in and ask for you, but Patrick's asleep and I'd hate to wake him."

"I'm at the training center. It's about a quarter mile east, on the same road. Can you see the sign from there?"

He peered into the brightness of the rising sun. "I think so. Stay put. I'm on my way."

The hair on the back of his neck prickled as he looked in the side-view mirror to check for on-coming traffic. There was nobody in sight, yet his senses remained on high alert, as they had been since the break-in. Every dark SUV seemed to be on his trail, not to mention a few other models and colors. The sensation was akin to driving on drifting sand that might be hiding an improvised explosive device. Yeah, been there, done that.

His focus shifted. *There she was!* Sight of the slim, dark-haired woman with a large dog at her side raised Sean's spirits immeasurably. How could he have forgotten how lovely his old friend was? How pleasing it was to be around her?

Zoe waved. Sean's heart beat faster. This reunion felt more like coming home than he'd imagined it would. He was older and wiser, of course. Well, at least older. If he'd been at all wise, he'd have realized how much Zoe had meant to him in the first place.

Cruising to a stop at the low curb, Sean sat behind the wheel and tried to regain control of his emotions. This wasn't another flashback of the kind that left him frightened and fearful. This was the kind that made him want to weep and wrap Zoe in an embrace that should be reserved for close family—or the woman he loved. She was neither, and yet...

Her grin was wide, her dark eyes sparkling. He didn't notice she was decked out in a police uniform and fully armed until he'd climbed out of the truck. Some men might have found that off-putting, but it pleased Sean greatly.

The decision of whether or not to hug her was taken from him the instant she threw herself into his arms. All he could do was hang on and blink back tears.

To his surprise and relief, her eyes were moist when she released him. She swiped at her cheeks, grinned and sniffled. "Bright sun will do this to me every time."

"Yeah. Me, too." He was so glad to see her he was nearly speechless. The urge to kiss her was too strong to resist, so he brushed his lips against her cheek before straightening to say, "You're looking good."

"Not so bad yourself," she countered with a blush. "You've packed on more muscle since we were in college."

"Compliments of Uncle Sam." His gaze drifted to his truck. "I wish I'd known before, what I know now."

"Yeah, well, time has a way of wising us up whether we like it or not."

"You never married?" he found himself asking.

Zoe laughed softly. "If you asked my chief back in Mesa, he'd say I'm married to my job. I like to think it's worth it." She sobered. "Did you have any trouble getting here?"

"Not that I know of. I kept thinking we were being followed, but it was probably my imagination. I tend to do that. If I hadn't actually fought with those two guys in my apartment, I'd be wondering if the attack was real."

"I asked the chief here, Ryder Hayes, to send for a copy of your incident report," Zoe said. "There wasn't much to it."

"Did it say whether there was news on the ballistics?"

"Not yet. Don't get discouraged. We'll keep an eye on your case."

He scanned her khaki uniform. "Are you working here?"

"Not today, but I do sub. Just getting the dog used to seeing me ready for duty and doing a bit of extra training. Why don't I get my car and you can follow me home. I'm sure you'd like to get Patrick settled and get some rest yourself."

"Home with you? I figured I'd rent a motel room."

"Don't be silly. I have plenty of space."

He eyed the panting dog at their feet. "What about your K-9? Will she be okay with a kid?"

"Yes, she'll be fine. That was part of her training. These dogs can differentiate between felons and friends."

Still concerned, Sean leaned closer to speak

more privately even though they were alone. "Patrick is not typical in any sense of the word, Zoe. We're going to have to be very careful when we introduce them. The poor kid has had it rough."

"I understand. I really do," she said. "But didn't his doctors warn against babying him too much?"

"Ensuring his safety is not the same thing. If those guys who broke into our apartment had seen him acting up, they might have shot him just to make him be quiet." Sean squelched a shiver. "When he gets scared and can't communicate, he tends to panic."

"Maybe Freya can help with that, too," Zoe said. "This evening, after supper, I'll invite my trainer and the K-9 cop who founded the assistance dog center to join us for coffee and dessert. That way Patrick won't have to sit through a whole meal with strangers if he isn't able, and they'll still get a good idea of your needs. Okay?"

"Sounds like you've worked it all out."

"I'm doing my best."

"I know you are." Starting to turn toward his truck he said, "Let's go. I'm ready."

Traffic was predictably light all the way to the rented house. The place was actually too big for one person but was all that had been available, so she'd leased it. Looking back, she wondered if God had arranged the extra room for this purpose. True or not, the notion was comforting.

She motioned Sean to pull into the driveway ahead of her. Instead, he drove onto the sorry excuse for a lawn and left room by the garage for her.

"I meant for you to use the driveway," she said, approaching his truck.

"It all looks the same to me."

"So I gathered. You parked on what's supposed to be the lawn when it gets proper watering."

"Sorry." An eyebrow arched. "Is it always this cold here? When I think of the desert, I picture heat."

"It depends on the elevation and time of year," Zoe said. "A light jacket is usually enough for us, even in the winter. When there's snow in Flagstaff and around the Grand Canyon, it can feel colder, though. It generally warms up during the day and cools off when the sun goes down."

She leaned to peer into his truck and smiled broadly at the little boy who'd just awakened. "You must be Patrick." When the child hid his face, she added, "My name is Zoe."

"That's right," Sean said. "This is the friend I told you about while we were driving. She's a very nice lady."

Still, the child cowered. "I'll go get my partner," she told Sean, adding a smile at Patrick. "Then we'll all go inside together."

Forcing the little boy to act sociable would have been wrong no matter what. Since he was clearly afraid, Zoe wanted to make certain this first meeting with her K-9 went smoothly. Therefore, she ordered Freya to heel and kept her on a short leash.

Sean was carrying Patrick and waiting at the front door of the simple, one-story, stucco home. The boy had his face pressed to his daddy's shoulder, hiding his eyes as if doing that made him invisible.

Sensing his uneasiness, the dog whined and wagged her tail. Zoe was about to silence her when she saw a big blue eye peeking out to see what was making the noise.

"This is Freya," Zoe said. "She lives and works with me. She's really friendly."

The key turned in the lock. Zoe pushed open the door and stood back. "After you."

A small hand reached back, and both of the child's eyes peered over Sean's shoulder. "Da."

"Dog? Yes, she's a dog. A very nice dog," Zoe said. "Would you like to meet her?"

"Da!"

Zoe laughed. "I think it's time you put Patrick down, Sean. He may not be ready to accept me," she whispered, "but it looks like he's more than ready to have a fur buddy."

"I don't know."

"Let's try it," she suggested. "Put Patrick down so he and Freya can meet on the same level." A flat hand in front of the eager K-9's muzzle kept her from lunging and overwhelming the child the way most dogs would.

As soon as the boy's shoes touched the floor he ducked behind his daddy's leg, holding on at the knee. Zoe wasn't worried. She caught Sean's eye and shook her head to keep him from interfering, then sat on her heels.

"Patrick, this is Freya." She looked to her panting partner. "Freya, this is Patrick. *Friend.*"

There was no doubt the dog agreed. Although she kept her distance as ordered, she began to wiggle as if seated on a hill of swarming ants.

"Put your hand out like this and let her sniff you," Zoe said, demonstrating. "She can tell you like her by the way your fingers smell."

Sean interrupted. "Is that true?"

"In a manner of speaking. She can sense fear and pick out gunpowder residue, plus all sorts of icky things I won't mention. The key is this introduction. It will be your turn as soon as Patrick is done."

"Maybe I should…"

"Trust me?" she said.

A soft chuckle preceded Sean's reply. "Since when did you get so bossy?"

"Since I was trained and know what I'm doing."

"Humph. Okay. You're the police officer."

"Yup," she said with an echoing laugh. "Watch and learn, civilian."

Another hand signal caused Freya to lie down.

Patrick reached forward. She sniffed his finger-tips, then licked them. He giggled. "Like me."

"Yes, she does. And so do I," Zoe said. As if on cue, the dog rolled over, tail still wagging, legs flopping wide. "She trusts you and wants you to scratch her tummy," Zoe told the boy. "Go ahead. Her fur is really soft."

He had to come out from behind Sean and squat to reach the dog's stomach. Zoe couldn't have been happier at his rapid response. She grinned up at Sean. "Okay. Your turn. She wouldn't have rolled over if she was worried about you, so join the party."

Sean began by crouching, then dropped all the way next to his son, keeping one arm around him. Patrick eased into his father's lap, followed closely by Freya. The idyllic scene was the kind that made Zoe wish she could snap a photo without disturbing them. Father and son were hugging each other while the dog leaned against Sean's chest and reached up to lick under his chin as if they had known each other for years.

He laughed. "As Patrick said, I think she likes me."

"I'd say so. It's a good thing her main training is in search and rescue. You might be ruining her if she was an attack dog."

"Really?"

Because he looked worried she admitted to

teasing. "No. Not really. But it is unusual to see her take to anybody so fast."

"She knows we're the good guys, right, Patrick?" Sean said. The boy nodded his agreement.

Zoe slowly rose. "Tell you what. After you put your things in your room and we go shopping for your favorite foods, maybe I'll have time to teach Patrick how to brush her. Would you like that, honey?"

Again a nod, this time with a shy smile. Zoe had no quarrel with his medical diagnosis. She simply saw more to Patrick's reticence than brain damage. In her opinion, he needed to be showered with love in order to be more confident, to blossom the way she felt he could.

Whether there would be time for her to help enough to matter was not up to her, it was up to her heavenly Father. She was beginning to suspect that Sean's need to come to Desert Valley was not limited to one objective. There was healing here for him. And for Patrick. And, God willing, for her, as well.

It had been a long time since she'd actually looked forward to having free time and not concentrating on her job 24/7. Truth to tell, she sort of felt like a puppy that had just been let out into a big play yard for the first time. If she hadn't been afraid of frightening Patrick she might have pumped a fist in the air and danced around the room.

THREE

After a quick tour of the house, Sean agreed to ride with Zoe and Freya rather than drive separately to the grocery store. If she had been anybody other than an armed police officer, he wasn't sure what he'd have done. He'd been so used to taking care of himself and being the only responsible adult in his son's life, it felt odd to not stay in full control.

She glanced over at him and smiled. "What's wrong?"

"Nothing."

"Right. And I'm Santa Claus. Talk to me, Murphy. I know something's bugging you."

Shrugging, he smiled at her. "Actually, I just realized I can relax a little when I'm with you. It's hard to accept."

"What is? Relaxing or trusting me?"

"Not being in command. Since I got back to the States, I've had to do it all. Believe me, the Shepherds didn't like most of my decisions."

"Such as?"

Sean lowered his voice and glanced over his shoulder at the backseat where his son and the dog were having a whispered conversation that included a lot of face licking on Freya's part. "Whether or not to bring Patrick home, for one. They wanted him to either stay in rehab or go to their house for private treatment. When I saw how unhappy he was in the hospital environment and how much better he acted with me, I decided to spring him."

"What did his therapists say?"

It hurt to repeat the negative opinions. "They felt he had made all the progress he probably would, and it didn't matter whether I left him there or took him with me."

"Then you have no reason to feel guilty." Zoe smiled. "Right?"

"Right. All I have to do is get my own act together so I can be a good father to him. If I keep having flashbacks, I may have to relinquish custody—for his sake."

"And give it to whom? I remember when your mom and dad were killed in that auto accident during my second semester of college." She arched her brows. "Surely you wouldn't consider your wife's parents after what you've told me!"

"No, no. Never them. They've already indicated that their idea of handling his problems is to overlook how much he needs love." Although he wanted to turn his face away and retreat, Sean remained stoic. "I had no idea how bad things had gotten while I was in the service. Sandra told me she'd gone home to her family's estate because she was lonely, not because she intended to stay stoned all the time and wanted Mommy and Daddy to watch Patrick."

"That's what happened?"

"Yeah."

"So, you asked for a discharge?"

"It wasn't that simple. I was on my way to the airport, ready to fly home because of Patrick's accident, when one of my buddies drove over an IED. The explosion took out half the Humvee and killed two men. I was thrown clear. By the time I got out of the hospital, I'd been diagnosed with PTSD, Sandra had died from an overdose and Patrick was still struggling to recover."

"Wow."

Sean nodded soberly. "Yeah. My sentiments exactly."

"You should be thankful you were able to get him away from your in-laws for this trip. I'm sure they didn't like it."

"I didn't tell them. They act as though I'm the reason for everything that went wrong." His jaw set. "Actually, they aren't the only ones. I had a long layover in Minneapolis during the trip home and used the time to pay a condolence visit to the family of one of the men who'd been with me in the Humvee. They slammed the door in my face. I guess they blamed me since they had no one else around to be mad at."

"I'm so sorry."

"As they say, 'No good deed goes unpunished,' right?"

Zoe pulled into the supermarket parking lot, found a space and turned to stare at him. "Could *they* have been responsible for sending the thugs to harm you?"

"I can't see why. Or how."

"What about Sandra's folks?"

"No. Violence is definitely not their way of handling problems. They have enough money to hire the best lawyers and sue for custody if they want me out of the picture."

He saw her hands fist on the steering wheel as she asked, "Do you think they might resort to that?"

"Unless I can get a grip on my flashbacks and prove I'm stable, it's a possibility. That's another reason why I need the help of a service dog. I've seen for myself what a difference one of those can make. Guys who were hardly able to leave their houses are working again and leading fairly normal lives."

"You managed to drive all the way down here. Are you sure you qualify?"

"I don't know whether I could have made myself act if it hadn't been for Patrick," Sean said flatly. "Whatever I did, I did for him. And that's what I'll keep doing for as long as I'm able."

She patted the back of his hand. "I believe you."

The grocery store was crowded. Zoe grabbed a cart, wiped it down to eliminate germs and stood back. "There you go, Patrick. All ready."

The child buried his face against his father's shoulder and clung to him.

"Wait right here," she said. "I'll be back in a sec."

There was no rule against taking her K-9 partner with her anywhere she went. She had left Freya in the car to simplify their shopping trip but could now see that had been a mistake. Freya was Patrick's temporary service dog, had been since the moment he'd laid a small hand on her back and let her lead him from room to room in the unfamiliar house.

A working vest identified Freya the way a badge gave Zoe authority. She buckled it on and the dog assumed a more cautious demeanor.

"Good girl. Heel."

Patrick's face lit with a smile. His eyes twinkled. "Da."

"That's right, Patrick," Zoe said. "The dog is coming with us. Can you show her how nicely you sit in the cart?"

She was afraid Sean might balk when it came time to let go. Thankfully, he didn't. Patrick's feet slipped through the leg openings, and he grasped the cart handle as if preparing to ride a bucking bronco.

"Freya will stay right here next to us while we shop," Zoe said. "Will you help me watch her to make sure she behaves?"

The child nodded. "Good da."

"That's right. She's a very good dog."

Sean took up a position on the side opposite the dog so they flanked the boy well. Zoe supposed she couldn't blame him for caution, but some of his choices seemed excessive. Maternal instinct kept insisting that there was no way any child could reach full potential when he or she was kept so close, so guarded, yet she could also identify with the urge to protect Patrick.

As they worked their way through the store, however, her opinion softened. Sean was gently but firmly requiring the boy to at least try to name whatever food he wanted them to buy. Truth to tell, she would have lost patience if she hadn't known how important the exercise was.

"I didn't think we were ever going to get those tangerines," she commented on their way to checkout. "You did a wonderful job working through the name."

"I watched the doctors," Sean said. "It seemed to me they were making things too simple until I realized that breaking the words into syllables was the way to go." He stepped ahead of her and took out his wallet. "Let me get this. Most of it's for us, anyway."

"I don't mind."

"I know. Humor me."

His smile warmed her cheeks enough that she backed off and let him pay. Freya stayed at the rear of the cart as they both bent to unload it. Zoe was concentrating so completely on Sean, it took her a few seconds to notice the dog's low growl. She grabbed his arm to still him and froze, herself.

His response was immediate, his voice raspy. "What?"

"The dog. Look."

Instead of facing them, tongue lolling and tail wagging, Freya had turned so that her back was to Patrick and the adults. She was staring past the next person in line and focusing on one of the aisles.

Zoe rested the heel of her hand on her holster and straightened. "You finish checking out while I go see what's wrong."

"No."

The command was so forceful, so packed with emotion, she stopped. He was right. If the dog was sensing danger and had put her back to them, then she was reacting to an unseen threat inside the store. As an off-duty police officer, it was still Zoe's duty to protect and serve. Should she protect her friends and serve the community by calling the station and reporting a possible problem? Maybe. The trouble was, without any visible threat she'd be out of line to do so. Nevertheless, she made the call.

Staying on full alert, Zoe kept her eye on her dog and the other shoppers while Sean loaded the bags in their cart and paid the cashier.

"Ready to go," he said behind her.

"Okay. You lead the way. Look for anybody from your past or things that seem unusual. I'll bring up the rear."

"It was dark when I was attacked in my apartment. I didn't get a good look at either of those guys."

"Doesn't matter," she said. "You know how to judge body language from being in combat. This isn't a lot different."

She heard him sigh before he said, "Yeah, providing I don't see an innocent person and read more into their posture than is really there."

"Better safe than sorry." As soon as the automatic door slid closed behind them she moved to shield the boy despite the fact that Freya had settled down.

Sean noticed. "Looks like the dog is okay now."

"Yes. The threat was apparently inside. Go ahead and load Patrick and the food into the car while I stand guard. We'll leave as soon as a local unit arrives."

"How soon will that be?"

"Hopefully, not long." She used her cell phone again, then told him, "ETA less than five."

"Why didn't you radio?"

"Because I'm not actually on duty now." Waving to an approaching patrol car she stepped away. "Here they are. Be right back."

Sean watched her jog across the parking lot to speak with the other officers. He'd managed to quell unreasonable fear inside the store and was feeling even less jittery now that they were out. Patrick was already in the backseat, as was the working dog. Some of the plastic grocery bags were piled on the floor while others shared the bench seat with the child and the K-9. Sean was surprised to see Freya sitting quietly instead of wiggling as before and stepping on perishables.

"Ah, you're still in uniform, aren't you," he muttered. "Of course. You think you're on duty."

At first, he assumed the dog's ensuing reaction was to his voice. She slowly rose, growling and bristling. The effect of her hair standing up made her look twice as big. And dangerous. But she wasn't looking at him. Or at his son. Again, she was focused beyond them.

"Zoe!" Sean shouted.

She whirled, her hand hovering over her holster. "What?"

Sean turned to follow the dog's line of sight. A beefy man wearing a dark vest was walking past in the distance. He could have been anybody. There was no reason for concern. Or was there?

By the time Zoe rejoined him at her car, the stranger had climbed into a dusty red pickup.

She touched Sean's arm. "Did you recognize somebody?"

"No." Frowning, he kept watching as the truck pulled away. "It was your dog again. She really doesn't like that guy in the dirty truck."

"She may have picked up the scent of gunpowder or drugs coming from him. Whatever is wrong, I'd trust her opinion over that of almost any human."

"Okay." Still peering at the truck, Sean caught his breath and reached for Zoe's arm. "Look!"

"What? What do you see that I don't?"

"The passenger," Sean gasped. "His arm. On the open window. It looks like it's in a cast!"

"Why would…?"

"Because I hit one of my attackers with Patrick's baseball bat. Remember?"

"You told me you fought them off. You never mentioned a bat." She was already running back to direct the patrol car. Those officers jumped into their unit and started in pursuit.

"Do you think they'll catch them?" Sean called as she returned.

A solemn shake of her head was all the answer he got. All he needed. Given the delay starting the pursuit, chances were not good.

"Sorry," Sean said. "I shouldn't have put Patrick in the car. I just thought it would be safer."

"It was. It is. I wouldn't have chased after them in a private vehicle, anyway. It's dangerous enough with red lights and sirens."

He nodded.

"Believe it or not, we don't usually go around acting wild like the cops on TV and in the movies. I have yet to take a class on how to jump onto the top of a speeding car and disarm the suspects inside."

"No?" Despite the recent fright, he couldn't help smiling slightly at the mental picture. "That's too bad. I'd have liked to watch."

"Then rent a DVD. I'm not doing any leaping."

"Not even to entertain Patrick?"

"No, but I do have some ideas for him. If we get you into a class soon, I can recommend a local day care. The police chief's daughter goes there, so you know it's very safe."

Sean had to take a deep breath before trying to answer. "I never thought about having to leave him. I figured he could stay with me. He'll behave. I know he will. Particularly if he gets to watch dogs."

"And not be allowed to play with them? I doubt it," Zoe said. "But let's not get ahead of ourselves. We still have to convince Ellen Foxcroft to put you in her program."

"You're right. One thing at a time," Sean said. "Let's go home."

"And keep an eye out for that red truck on the way."

"Oh, yeah." He had already buckled up and was braced to keep watch, front and rear.

Had the would-be assassins really tracked him here? Were they that clever? Was he that careless? He hadn't thought so, but it was beginning to look as if the danger he'd wanted to escape was still with him.

If only he knew why somebody wanted him dead. Knowing *why* might point him to *who* and he'd know what to do next. There had to be something. There had to be. He needed to survive for Patrick's sake. Surely God wouldn't punish an innocent child for the mistakes of his parents.

If he still believed in the power of prayer, he might reach out. Beg for protection for his son. However, he had prayed repeatedly for Sandra's redemption and look what the result had been. How could he trust a God who let a child nearly drown? Who deprived the boy of a mother?

That thought brought him up short. In the case of Sandra's untimely death, perhaps that was the only thing that had protected Patrick from her drug-induced mania. But then the pool. Why the pool?

Sean's mind was whirling, stunned by myriad possibilities, none of which made sense to him. He was a civilian now, ready to take care of his son, but he wasn't whole, either. How could a loving heavenly Father expect to use an earthly father who was so damaged?

And then it hit him. Without Patrick, without purpose, there would be no reason to fight anymore. No reason to try to heal. No reason to have come to Desert Valley, to have reunited with the extraordinary woman seated beside him.

He gazed at Zoe. Right now, he needed her help. Maybe, when all this was over, he'd be able to repay her kindness. He certainly hoped so because now that he had seen her again, he didn't intend to let more long years pass without keeping in closer touch. If he had not had her to reach out to when his life fell apart recently he didn't know how he'd have managed.

Something flashed in the rays of the setting sun, as if glinting off a gun barrel. Sean yelled. Ducked. Unsnapped his seat belt and threw himself over the back of his seat toward Patrick just as a shot rang out.

Freya closed her mouth on Sean's shoulder to stop him but didn't bite hard enough to break the skin.

Zoe swerved toward the curb. "Anybody hit?"

"No," he shouted. "I saw a reflection just in time. Get us out of here!"

"Hang on!"

Temporarily steering with one hand, she punched a button on her cell phone. "Trent here. Possible shots fired. We're almost to my house. It's the old Peterson place on Second, not far from Sophie Williams's. We took fire about a half-mile south. Can't pinpoint the exact location."

Sean barely had hold of the buckle on his seat belt when she dropped the phone and fisted both hands tightly on the wheel. Her jaw was set.

"What did they say?"

"They're on the scene. Found the red truck, abandoned, close to where we were shot at. It was stolen. If the guys took off on foot, they were probably our shooters."

"That makes sense."

"Maybe. Maybe not. Either way, I'm getting you and Patrick back inside where you'll be safer. They can't hit you if they can't see you."

"I'm sorry I dragged you into this," Sean said.

"You didn't drag me into anything. I walked in with both eyes open. This is what I do. Why I got into this business. What good is all my special training if I don't use it?"

He recalled one silly way they used to tease each other in college and revived it, hoping his breathlessness wasn't too evident. "So, where's your superhero cape?"

"At the cleaner's," she shot back as she slid the

car around a tight corner in perfect control. "I use a badge and a gun, now."

Sean sighed. "That's my Zoe. Saving the world, one friend at a time."

He wasn't happy with the role reversal. Men were supposed to rescue damsels in distress. He snorted quietly. That was not likely to happen when the woman in question was his old friend, Zoe Trent.

FOUR

Zoe didn't slow much as she entered the open garage. If she hadn't been concerned about the whole situation, she might have laughed when Sean braced himself on the dash with both hands.

"I've been taught defensive driving," she said. "Don't panic."

"Defensive is one thing. Driving through the back wall of a garage is another."

"Ya think?" A soft chuckle erupted. "Don't worry. I have complete control."

"So you say. If you don't mind, I'll get out now."

"I don't mind a bit." She was lowering the mechanized garage door behind them with the push of a button. "This side door to the house isn't locked. Go on in with Patrick. I'll bring Freya and the groceries."

"You get the dog. I'll get the food."

"Now who's being bossy?"

"I am." He'd already bent and picked up his son

when she joined him and asked, "Is there a problem with his motor skills, too?"

"Some. Why?"

"Because I thought it would be good for him to walk more. He can lean on Freya again if he needs support."

"He falls easily."

"And how did he learn to walk in the first place?"

She noted Sean's sigh. Perhaps she was being too outspoken. Then again, maybe bluntness was just what he needed. It was possible to love someone or something so much you didn't give it the opportunity to learn and grow. The same was true of the canines in the various programs. If they weren't pushed, they'd not only fail to make progress, they might regress. Training was a daily necessity, as was affection. Each had its place and time.

Leading the way, Zoe entered with the dog at her heels, leaving the door open behind them. When she turned, Sean was gently lowering Patrick to the floor and bending to speak to him.

"I'll be right back, buddy. I have to go get your tangerines and the other stuff we bought. You watch the dog for us like you did at the store, okay?"

The tousled, blond head nodded without hesitation. "Good da."

"Dog." Sean put emphasis on the final letter. "Daw—guh."

To Zoe's surprise and joy, Patrick repeated it perfectly. She would have cheered if she hadn't seen moisture gleaming in his father's eyes. Every small step was a triumph, every properly annunciated word a victory.

"Thank You, Lord, for letting me be a part of this amazing healing process," she whispered, blinking back her own tears. She'd thought her offer of assistance was meant for one person, and it was actually going to benefit at least two.

Make that three, she added. Not only had her heavenly Father reunited dear friends, He had placed her in a position to render aid and share blessings. No amount of threat, no lowlife with an evil agenda, was going to steal that from her. Not now. Not ever again.

The scheduled visit with lead K-9 trainer, Sophie Williams, and Ellen Foxcroft, the founder of the assistance dog program, took place as scheduled at Zoe's house. Sean liked both women, and Zoe's introduction of him and his disabled son wasn't maudlin. As a matter of fact, it was so uplifting he wondered if she'd talked her associates right out of helping him.

"I never claimed to be totally helpless," he told the women with a nod toward Patrick. "But as you can see, there are special circumstances. I not only need to be able to function for my own sake, I need to be there for my son. As much as it pains me to admit it, I'm not myself." His elbows were propped on his knees, his hands joined between them while he toyed with his wedding band.

Ellen mirrored his pose. Her reddish hair hung in a single braid down her back. Her gaze was tender. "I know how hard this is for you, Mr. Murphy. The human body sometimes deals with intense trauma in ways that go against everything we expect. That doesn't make us less of a person. It's how we cope with the aftereffects of disaster that will define who and what we become. By asking for help you've taken a big step, and I want to tell you how impressed I am."

"Just get me well for Patrick," Sean said with passion. "I don't care what it takes. Whatever I have to do, I'll do it. I promise."

"I know you will." She glanced at Sophie. "What do you think of giving Angel another chance?"

The lead trainer smiled and shook her head. "It's easy to see why the folks who donated her named her Ding-a-ling. She really is a sweetheart, but do you really think she's salvageable?"

Zoe had been fidgeting. Now she spoke up. "Why Angel? I mean, she's lovable and partially trained in several disciplines, but she's also terribly headstrong and easily distracted."

"Exactly why she needs a strong, forceful, determined man as her partner," Ellen replied. "Mr. Murphy is right about not being as badly affected as many of our clients, so why not let him give Angel a try? It's that or wash her out of all our programs."

Watching his old friend's expression, Sean could tell she was mulling over the suggestion. A misfit dog for a misfit soldier. What could be better?

Zoe finally nodded. "Okay. How can I help?"

"We'll do introductions first thing in the morning. Bring everybody involved to the training center with you but don't wear your uniform. We want that meeting to be as casual as possible so we can judge Angel's reactions. If she passes that test, we'll make up a training schedule."

The women stood, as did Sean. "Thank you, both," he said.

Sophie nodded and shook Sean's hand, then paused and looked to Zoe. "By the way, what was the disturbance at the market all about? I understand from Ryder that a threat may have followed Mr. Murphy to Desert Valley, after all."

Sean knew she was referring to the chief of police, Ryder Hayes, the same person who had sent for the report about his break-in back in St. Louis.

"It started when I thought I saw somebody who had caused me trouble in St. Louis," Sean explained. "It turned out they were driving a stolen truck and ditched it right before somebody took a potshot at Zoe's car."

Ellen nodded. "I heard we tried using James Harrison's bloodhound, but he lost their trail. Do you think the incidents were connected?"

"I'm sure beginning to," Zoe said. "Freya reacted to one of the guys when we were all in the store."

Sophie nodded. "We'll all need to be on alert. See you tomorrow morning at eight."

Sean hung back as Zoe walked her friends to the door. Patrick had curled up on the sofa with Freya. The dog opened one eye, studied him for a second, then closed it, sighed and relaxed. If the new dog he was about to meet was half the canine companion Freya was, he'd be more than satisfied.

It suddenly struck him that canine senses were going to be the answer. If he felt threatened and the dog did not, then he'd know his imagination was in charge. If, however, the dog reacted as well, he could begin to trust his own senses. To trust himself.

What might it be like to actually lighten up and enjoy life again? Considering the way he'd been feeling, the concept sounded both enticing and out of reach.

Sean shivered, remembering the words of his attackers. They had been sent to kill him. That was all there was to it. If they were here, in Desert Valley, there was no way he'd ever be able to let down his guard. Not if he expected to live long enough to raise his child.

Zoe took a brief phone call later in the evening. She'd watched the tension building on her friend's face as she'd listened, so the first thing she did was set Sean's mind at ease. "That was Chief Hayes."

"What now?"

"Good news, actually," she said, smiling. "They were able to get usable prints off that stolen red truck. They belonged to local kids who have been in trouble here before, not hit men from St. Louis."

"They're sure?"

"Positive."

"But, the guy we saw in the parking lot was no kid."

"Maybe. Maybe not. In any case, they're also running a partial palm print through the AFIS database to see if there are any matches."

It pained her to see some of the starch go out of Sean's spine. "You can't convince me it's all in my head, so don't even try."

"That's not what I meant. We didn't find any shell casings today, but the bullet in your apartment ceiling was plenty real."

"True. I wish I had a better idea of who has it in for me. I haven't been home long enough to have made new enemies, so it has to be somebody from my past."

"Or Sandra's," Zoe said. "Did you pick up any of her stuff from her parents?"

"Nothing except clothes for Patrick and a few toys."

"Could she have hidden drugs in those?"

"If she did, the proof is back in my old apartment. I left too fast to take much with me."

"I could have Chief Hayes contact the St. Louis department and suggest they do a thorough search. The problem is, if they do turn up illicit drugs, it will look as if you were hiding them."

"I hadn't thought of that."

Zoe shrugged. "At this time it's a moot point. Anybody who thought you were hiding drugs has probably already ransacked the place. You can check when you're done training here and then involve the police if you need to after Christmas. In the meantime I'll be keeping careful watch, just in case. So will my colleagues."

"Mentioning Christmas reminds me," Sean said. "I can understand why you haven't put up holiday decorations, but would you mind if I did a few things for Patrick?"

She clapped her hands. "I'd love it! I wasn't even considering Christmas when I left Mesa in September."

"Do you know where we can get a tree?"

"I do. The church youth are having a sale. And rehearsals are starting for the outdoor Christmas pageant, too. We can get Patrick involved in that when we go to church on Sunday."

The off-putting look on his face was disappointing. "We don't go to church."

She made a face. "Why not? You used to."

"Things change. People change." He lowered his voice to add, "I've changed."

"Fine. God hasn't. And whether you admit it or not, your little boy needs to learn about faith. If you won't go with us, Freya and I will take him."

"I could stop you."

"You could try." Although she no longer wore her holster or uniform, she struck a dominant pose, feet apart, hands fisted on the hips of her jeans, shoulders back. Yes, she was being pushy. And, yes, Patrick was Sean's responsibility. But she cared so much for both of them it was hard to stand back when she thought there was something she could do or say that would help.

"You're actually serious." Sean was frowning.

"You're right. I am."

"Okay, I'll think about it."

"You do that. And while you do, I'll be praying that you come to your senses."

"Why do you think faith makes sense?"

Zoe began to smile. "The very definition of faith is belief without seeing. You had it once." She jabbed a finger at his chest. "It's still in there. All you have to do is look."

"I have," Sean argued.

She wasn't about to back down. Not when she was convinced he needed his former faith in order to complete his healing. "If I could loan you some of mine I would, but it's an inside job. You can't borrow it or catch it like a cold. You have to seek the Lord yourself."

"God gave up on me long ago," Sean said flatly.

Zoe couldn't help smiling. Instead of continuing to argue, she merely said, "Then you might want to ask how you got here and why you escaped death when the bomb went off on your way to the airport and when those guys tried to kill you in St. Louis and since then, because it seems to me He's rescued you over and over lately."

The expression on her old friend's face was painful to look at when he focused on his only child and said, "I'd gladly have traded those supposed rescues for Patrick's well-being."

Why *did* bad things happen? She had no idea. But she was certain of one thing. The only way she'd have survived the tragic loss of her baby brother was through a belief that they would someday be reunited in heaven.

And in the meantime, she intended to stand up for earthly justice as best she could. It was foolish to try to discern divine wisdom or assume she could figure out everything that was occurring. All she knew for sure was that she was glad Sean had come to her and brought his son. Anything beyond that would work out for the best.

Zoe didn't know why she was so positive, but she wasn't about to argue with her conclusions. If it became necessary for her to act as the law enforcement officer she was, then so be it. Rookie or not, she was ready.

Mulling over the recent call about the fingerprints in the stolen truck, she realized Sean was right. The figure they had seen get into it was no teenager. He'd not only looked like an adult, he'd moved like one. Heavy. Purposeful.

Dangerous? Maybe. Probably. She felt a shiver climb her spine like a squirrel skittering up the trunk of a ponderosa pine. At the same time she was encouraging Sean to relax, she was going to have to double her guard. And keep him from realizing it.

FIVE

Their first stop the following morning was to be the training center. Sean had made pancakes for all of them while Zoe tended to the coffee and helped Patrick dress. He had only allowed her to assist the boy because the doctors had recommended changing off caregivers to encourage independence. It had apparently worked because when she entered the kitchen, Patrick was holding her hand and walking. His gait was stiff and somewhat awkward, but he seemed far more capable than previously.

"We came for pancakes." Zoe helped the boy into a chair and tucked a napkin under his chin.

When she paused and looked to Patrick, Sean heard him say, "Please."

"My pleasure." Deeply moved, Sean was turning away to tend the stove when his son added, "Please, Dad-dy." The frying pan faded for a moment while he regained control of his emotions.

When he looked back at the table, Zoe was beaming. "Good, huh?"

"Very good. Thanks for helping."

"Freya helped, too. She pulled on the toes of his socks while he tried to put them on. Patrick had to really fight to get them up."

"By himself?" Sean was astonished.

"Yup. All by himself."

"That's wonderful."

Zoe joined him at the stove. "Why don't you let me finish cooking while you two eat? I'm used to grabbing a quick cup of coffee and whatever I can chew on the run."

"Are we in a hurry?" Sean asked, suspicious.

"You do want to get started with your new dog, don't you?"

His brows knit. "Yes. But I'm getting the idea that there's more to your suggestion than you're letting on. What is it?"

"Nothing. Just..."

"Just what, Zoe?" Instead of going to the table, he lingered close to her. "You may as well tell me. I'm not going to eat a bite until you do."

"All right." As she raised her face, he saw concern mirrored in the dark depths of her eyes. "They got a hit on the ballistics from the bullet fired in your apartment."

"And?"

"And that gun had been used before. In multiple murders. Whoever came after you was no novice, even if he did behave like one that night."

"Hit men? Somebody sent professional hit men after me? Why?"

"It's anybody's guess," she said. "The only good thing about the information is that they're unlikely to have left the metropolitan area and followed you here."

If she had not been trembling slightly, Sean might have felt more comforted by her conclusion. Taking her elbow, he guided her to the table and urged her into one of the chairs. "Sit. I'll bring you breakfast. And then we'll go get my dog so I can be on my way."

"It doesn't work like that," she insisted. "If you're paired with one of Ellen's assistance dogs, you have to stay in Desert Valley for training."

Sean hesitated. Of course he had to stay. There was no way he'd get the help he needed unless he played by the rules. He filled three plates and delivered them to the table, then busied himself cutting Patrick's food into bite-size pieces while he processed his dilemma.

"I see your point," he finally said. "And I suppose it won't help if I keep running. I was just trying to remove the danger from around you."

"I'm not the one you should be worrying about," she said. "After we see how Angel reacts to Patrick, we'll take Patrick to the day care that I think is best."

"I don't want…"

"I know. You don't want him away from you for

a second. I get it. I do. But he'll be safer mixed in with other kids than he is if he stays with you all the time. You're the target, he isn't."

"Apparently. I just wish I knew why. The only important thing in my life is my son."

Zoe frowned. "As far as you know. There has to be something else going on. Someone hired the hit men for a reason. And the guys who are after you seem to be high-end. Who do you know with money to burn?"

"Sandra's parents, Alice and John Shepherd. But like I said, they'd hire a lawyer, not a thug."

"If you say so." She stuffed a bite of pancake into her mouth and licked her lips, momentarily distracting Sean and making him wonder what it would feel like to kiss that sweet mouth for real instead of only in his imagination. Shaking off the unwarranted thought, he said, "Okay. You're right. We'll go visit the day care. But I won't promise I'll leave him."

"Fair enough." Zoe licked her lips again, then reached for his mug. "More coffee?"

Sean was still staring at her tender, sweet mouth. "Huh?"

"Pay attention, Murphy. Do you want a refill?"

Sean merely nodded. He'd been paying attention, all right. To the wrong thing. The more time he spent with Zoe, the more he realized what a fool he had been to marry Sandra. He'd apparently been deluded by his youthful desires and had made the biggest mistake of his life; one it was too late to correct.

Or was it? Studying Zoe and admitting his own shortcomings, he concluded they would never be a good match. Not now. Not when she was so capable and he was damaged goods. Sadly, their chance for happiness had passed. He was simply pleased she'd stepped into his life long enough to render the kind of specialized aid for which she'd been trained.

Those thoughts led him further into the doldrums and left him wondering if she would consider looking after Patrick if something bad happened to him. It wasn't fair to even suggest it, of course, yet he desperately wanted to be able to count on someone he trusted. To know his son would be loved and cared for if the assassins finally succeeded.

Maybe later he'd bring up the subject, Sean decided. If he lived long enough.

A gentle touch on his arm drew him back to the present. Zoe had put down his steaming mug and was leaning closer, staring as if he'd just had an episode of regression. If he turned his head just a little, maybe…

"Earth to Murphy. Are you all right?"

"Fine." He swallowed hard. "Thanks for the coffee."

"Where were you just now? You didn't seem to be fighting a war again."

"Not the shooting kind." He laid his hand over hers and lowered his voice to speak more privately while Patrick happily stuffed himself, ignoring the adults. "I was just imagining the future if something happened to me."

"Well, something won't, so cut it out."

"If something did—" he cleared his throat and continued in a hoarse whisper "—would you consider becoming Patrick's guardian?"

"Me?"

"I know it's a lot to ask, but…"

"I'm not refusing. I'm touched, that's all." She eyed the content child and smiled. "He's the most important person in your whole life and you're offering to trust me to take care of him. Of course I'd do it." She placed her free hand over where theirs were joined, and sniffled.

The moisture glistening in her eyes brought a similar reaction in his as he said, "Thank you."

Next to them, grinning and sticky with syrup, Patrick giggled and echoed, "Tank you," interrupting their moving exchange and destroying the romantic mood.

Zoe recovered first, pulled away and pointed to the boy. "Your daddy will clean you up while I clear the table."

"I will?" Sean lifted an eyebrow.

"Oh, yeah. I may have offered to look after him in an emergency, but I'm not starting now. You fed him pancakes, so you get to wash off the sticky."

"You drive a hard bargain, Officer Trent."

She laughed. "You'd better believe it."

Sobering, Sean lifted his son into his arms. "You meant what you said? You'll step in if…"

"Absolutely. And if you're as serious about it as I am, we need to see an attorney and make it official."

It occurred to him to tease about marrying her, instead, then decided it would be cruel to even suggest such a thing. He was not going to place her in an untenable position, nor was he going to take the chance she might actually agree, for Patrick's sake.

"Fine," Sean said, as he left the kitchen. "You make the arrangements, and I'll keep my head down until it's legal."

"You'd better plan on keeping it down a lot longer than that," Zoe shouted after him. "I understand puppies a lot better than I understand little kids."

It was a delight to tour the training facility with Patrick. Every dog excited him, especially the pups he saw when Zoe kenneled Freya.

Crouching, she pointed to a pile of K-9 vests. "Remember how Freya acted different when she was wearing a police jacket and badge like those? Some of the dogs we have here are not very friendly even when they aren't all dressed up, so you shouldn't try to pet them without asking first. Understand?"

Patrick's head bobbed, his expression solemn. "Uh-huh."

"Good. Now let's go find my friends." She stood and offered her hand. "We need to introduce you and your daddy to Angel."

Judging by the way his eyes widened and he tugged on her hand, Zoe assumed the reference had confused him. She explained. "That's her name, honey. She's not a real angel, like in the Bible."

He seemed to be searching for a word. "Wings?"

"No, Patrick. No wings. She's just a really sweet dog. Come on. The trainers are waiting for us."

A wry smile on Sean's face reminded her that Sophie and Ellen had warned him about possible problems. If he wasn't open to accepting Angel, Zoe wasn't sure he'd have a second chance. Of course, he wasn't the only one who needed to display camaraderie. The dog's reactions were as important as the human's.

"I'll take care of Patrick for a few minutes while you go with Ellen," Zoe said as soon as pleasantries had been exchanged. "We'll be right out here, watching."

He eyed her casual attire. "You're not armed today."

"Not visibly. This place is always full of officers, so there's no need to worry. Most of the previous rookie class is still here, working for the DVPD, and some of those in my group stayed over to sub so officers like Shane Weston could go home to Flagstaff for Christmas. I think you'll like Tristan McKeller when you meet him, too. I mentioned him—he's a former soldier, same as you."

"The same? I doubt that." He hesitated. "You do understand why I won't carry a gun, right?"

"Because you don't want to have a flashback episode and make a terrible mistake. I get it. But if you think about all that's happened here and the way you've been protected, you'll see there's no need to be armed."

"I suppose gut feelings don't count."

"Not if they're yours. Sorry," she said, smiling to soften the comment even more. "Give it time. Heal. Work through your nervousness with a service dog by your side. Then you won't even want to be armed."

Sean sighed noisily. "I hope you're right."

"Haven't you heard? I am *always* right." Nudging him through the doorway after Ellen, she lifted Patrick and balanced him on her hip. "Wow. You're heavy today. Must be from all the pancakes you ate."

"Uh-huh."

As his small arms circled her neck and squeezed, Zoe felt a surge of emotion she had not anticipated. He was all shampoo and soap and syrup and…and love. How had that happened?

She'd liked him from their first meeting but had attributed those feelings to her friendship with his father. This was different. This was personal. And very dear.

Toting Patrick to the one-way viewing window, she told him to watch while his daddy met the dog that might provide their deliverance. Having a bond develop during an initial meeting was iffy, at best. The quirk on Angel's side was her over-abundance of love. She could track fairly well, but was more likely to lick a criminal she appre-hended than to growl or bite him as she was sup-posed to. That was what had ultimately washed her out of the K-9 cop program.

Sean was seated in a chair in the center of the room. A side door opened. Sophie started to lead Angel in and was almost jerked off her feet when the dog realized there were other people present.

"You may as well release her," Zoe heard Ellen say.

"Da!" Patrick didn't take his eyes off the leap-ing, dancing, pulling canine. "Da-gh."

Zoe gave him a squeeze. "That's right. Dog. Very good."

"Daddy."

Tears pooled in Zoe's eyes as she watched the scene unfold. Unleashed, Angel left the trainer at a run, made a dash to Sean and almost knocked him over backward, chair and all, when she tried to jump into his lap.

Of course he did everything wrong after that, including hugging the affectionate dog and letting her lick his face. She made several circles around the room, her nails scrambling on the slick floor, then returned to him to greet him with more exuberance.

All Zoe could do was whisper, "Thank You, Jesus," and swipe at her damp cheeks. They still had a lot of work ahead of them, but Sean and Patrick Murphy had their service dog. They would be staying in Desert Valley for training.

The two trainers had managed to corral Angel, fit her with a working harness and put her back on a long leash so Sean could walk her in the fenced training yard.

"How did you know she'd take to my son so fast?" Sean asked Zoe.

"She loves everybody. That's her problem. She'd rather give and receive affection than settle down and work."

"And that makes her good for me how?"

"We'll have to wait and see. If she forms a strong enough bond with your family, she may naturally provide protection."

"Suppose she doesn't. What then?"

Zoe surprised him with a sock on his shoulder. The dog was so busy wiggling and trying to lick Patrick's face she didn't even seem to notice the playful blow.

"Hey. What did you hit me for?"

"Because of your rotten attitude. How can you expect good results when you think so negatively?" She waved her hands in front of him as if erasing the comment. "Never mind. Forget it."

Watching the interaction between Angel and the boy, Sean realized she had a valid point. "You're right. I was being a downer. Sorry. It's just…"

"I know. Let's take it one day at a time." She eyed the happy dog. "This morning is off to a great start."

"Can I let her go soon?"

"Why? Don't you like being pulled along like a musher on a sled in Alaska?"

"Not particularly. I know Ellen said she needed a strong man to control her, but doesn't she ever quiet down?"

"Actually, letting her run off some of that excess energy might be good." Zoe grabbed the leash near the harness and firmly commanded, "Sit."

Angel plunked down, trembling with excitement but sitting all the same. As soon as the clasp clicked, she tried to bolt, but Zoe still had hold of the harness. In a few seconds she gave the command of release.

Patrick clapped his hands as his new furry friend took off in a dead run, circling him as if corralling a herd of sheep.

"That's natural instinct," Zoe said. "Angel was

a rescue. Her former owners insisted she was incorrigible. Because border collies are known for their intelligence, Sophie decided to put her in training and give her a chance."

"It's going to be hard to find her some sheep to chase around in St. Louis." As soon as he'd mentioned his former home, he saw Zoe's smile vanish. He didn't blame her. Thinking about their parting didn't make him happy, either. She was right about his mind-set, though. He needed to keep up his spirits for everyone's sake, especially Patrick's.

Forcing a wide smile, he tried to encourage his old friend. "Maybe I should buy a ranch."

Her brows arched. "Can you afford one?"

"No. Sandra kept insisting she had some kind of a trust fund to fall back on, but she never proved it to me. I imagine it was the drugs talking. If she'd had money, she could have gone anywhere instead of complaining about the housing I had provided on base and moving in with her parents."

"Did you ask them about it?"

"No way. They already thought I married her because they were wealthy. The last thing I want to do is mention piles of money, particularly before I get back on my feet and get a job to supplement my temporary disability." He shaded his eyes to watch the dog, saw her circle again and head straight for Patrick.

The boy opened his arms. Angel plowed into

him and sent him sprawling. With an angry shout, Sean raced to the boy and tried to shove her away.

Instead of giving ground, however, she stood fast, feet braced and curled a lip at him while Patrick laughed so hard he was gasping for breath.

"Stop," Zoe ordered. "Freeze. Look at the dog."

Sean rocked back on his heels once he realized the child was unhurt. "What's she doing?"

"Protecting him. From you. You came at him shouting, and she sensed you were upset so she stood guard."

"She's supposed to look out for me, too."

"I think she will, once you two have bonded more. Right now, I want to tell Ellen what just happened." She pulled out her cell phone. "This is amazing!"

As Sean relaxed and dropped into a sitting position beside the dog and child, he saw the canine back off, too. Given that he wanted to help Patrick as much as himself, he couldn't argue with what he'd just seen. If Zoe was pleased, so was he.

Deep breaths calmed him further. Scanning the yard, he noticed obstacles and jumps and all sorts of strange contraptions that he assumed were part of the training regimen. As soon as Zoe finished reporting to the service dog trainer, he planned to ask her how the equipment was used.

Definite joy filled her conversation. "That's right. She stopped to defend Patrick. I know. It's wonderful. Okay, we'll…"

When she broke off in midsentence Sean turned to look at her. Saw her pointing. Whipped around to follow her line of sight.

"The west fence," Zoe continued, this time cupping a hand over the phone to mute her words. "There's a guy standing out there now. He looks just like the man in the stolen red truck, the one they chased near the grocery store!"

SIX

Zoe wished she'd worn her Glock and had Freya by her side. The best she could do was corral everybody and move them inside. According to what she'd been told about the trouble in town back in August, assailants had arrived in a car and shot at Sophie with a rifle. At least this guy was on foot and had no visible weapon. If he'd been closer, she'd have drawn her concealed Ruger .380, but at this distance she might as well throw rocks.

Running up to Sean she shouted, "Inside. Now!"

"What's wrong?"

"I'm not sure. Just move."

Sean was already on his feet and scooping up his son.

She could tell by his expression that he was going to follow her orders. "Hurry!"

"What about the dog?"

He needn't have asked. Angel was right on his heels.

Zoe slammed the door. Breathless, she took a

moment to regain the proper demeanor. A police officer was supposed to remain calm in a crisis, rookie or not. "There was somebody loitering out by the farthest fence," she explained. "We had a shooting incident in the training yard about four months ago, and I didn't want to take a chance this time."

"Thanks, I think." He, too, acted out of breath. "You could have told me with a little less drama. You scared me good."

"Badly. I scared you badly."

Sean huffed and shook his head. "Those aren't the first words that popped into my head, believe me." He eyed his son. "I cleaned it up for both of you."

"Good." She went to one of the windows and peeked through the blinds. "I don't see him now."

"I never did. What did he look like?"

"One of the guys at the market that made you so nervous," Zoe said. "I thought for sure you'd seen him standing there."

"Nope. I was watching the dog until I heard you holler. After that, it's a blur."

"Well, at least you didn't have a flashback." She studied him. "You didn't, did you?"

"No. I didn't." He seemed both pleased and concerned. "I can't get well before we qualify for Angel."

"I'm sure it won't happen quickly. You just didn't have the right triggers this time. Besides, there's an outside chance Patrick can also qualify. You won't need two service dogs."

"True." He joined her to peer out the window as red-and-blue flashing lights reflected off the glass. "Is that every patrol car in Desert Valley?"

"Looks like it. We have so little crime around here the officers tend to respond whenever they can."

"You said there was a serial killer?"

"Not anymore. It's a long story. The former police department secretary turned out to be a psycho who was targeting cops. She was mentally unbalanced and thought she could make Chief Hayes fall in love with her if she got rid of all her rivals. In the process, she also killed officers who happened to resemble him because they didn't ask her for a date. It was a nightmare."

"Sounds like it." Sean stepped back. "I've been thinking. Since nobody has bothered Patrick, how about we take him to that day care you mentioned? I suspect you're right about him being safer if he's not around me."

"Granted. And I'll stop by the house for my other gun." She displayed the Ruger .380 in her palm. "This is only for close quarters."

Sean visibly tensed. "You'll keep it locked up when Patrick is around, right?"

"Absolutely. And I'll make sure it's unloaded."

"What do we do with the dog while we're gone?"

"It's about time you started using her name instead of calling her *the dog*. Angel will go with us, in a portable kennel, and I'll have Freya ride next to her to set a good example. You'd be surprised how much a smart dog can learn by observation."

Sean chuckled as he eyed the still-excited canine. "What makes you think Freya won't learn to act up from watching Angel?"

"I'll take my chances," Zoe said, returning his smile. She knew he was referring to the dogs, yet her reply had a double meaning. She was beginning to realize she might be willing to take a chance on caring for Sean again, too. He may have broken her heart once, but he wasn't the same macho guy he had been. What he needed to realize was that his inner strength was still there, still evident in his actions to protect his son. He wasn't less of a man than he had been. He was merely a wounded warrior whose invisible scars needed the balm of love and faith, both in himself and in the God he had recently denied.

It was her fondest hope that she could lead him back to a realization of both. She wasn't fooling herself. Her goals were not nearly as noble as they sounded because she had a vested interest in this matter, too.

She cared for the man deeply. They had both been through a lot since their youth. Above all, she was going to make sure he stayed safe, no matter what it took.

* * *

Sean's first opinion of Desert Valley Day care was not particularly good. It looked more like the usual private home, decorated for Christmas, than a professional place. There was a wreath on the front door, and twinkling lights hung from the porch, just like every other house on the block.

Meeting the two main caretakers, however, helped set his mind at ease. Marilyn Carter and her niece, Josie Callahan, had achieved a welcoming, family atmosphere and were offering sensible parental guidance to the children without a lot of unnecessary shouting.

The roomful of kids was noisy, of course. Most were younger, like Patrick. A brunette, dusky, blue-eyed girl of about ten stood in the background, acting as if she considered herself everyone's big sister. She was helping younger kids build a castle with blocks and gently admonishing them to share.

He inclined his head toward the group of children and spoke to Zoe. "Who's that? She looks old for day care."

"Maisy is Officer Dalton West's daughter. She's here after school because he's been in K-9 training classes, too," Zoe said. "Dalton is staying in Desert Valley over Christmas vacation, so she'll probably be here a lot."

"Maisy will make a good teacher someday," Josie added, sounding wistful.

Zoe sobered. "I suppose she tends to mother the little ones more because she lost her own mother."

Sean laid his hand on Patrick's head while the boy leaned against him. "I understand. It's hard."

Josie nodded and began to smile. "That's why Aunt Marilyn and I stay open so late and accept parents' flexible schedules. We know what a struggle it can be."

"Do you have children?" Sean asked.

"No, but Marilyn does." She turned away. "If you'll excuse me, I need to check the bathrooms."

"And I suppose I'll need to fill out enrollment paperwork." Sean looked to Zoe. "Can I use your address?"

"Sure." She paused. "It would be a good idea if you agreed to put Patrick in Sunday school, too. That way everybody can get to know you and feel more comfortable with you guys being a part of the day care."

"Sunday school? I gather you'll want me to go to church with you, too."

"Well…"

"I get it." Sean sighed noisily. "All right. You win. Church it is, but don't expect me to suddenly go running down the aisle and repent. God gave up on me long ago."

"Whatever you say."

He could tell she didn't mean it. Nevertheless, he would try to make things easier for her while he was there. She had opened her home and arranged for his training. The least he could do was go to church with her.

But it would be hard, he knew. Facing the faith he had rejected and being bombarded with pleas to reconsider was liable to creep into his mind and cause untold problems and spiritual confusion.

How did he know? Because it already was.

Zoe was glad to see Patrick being assimilated into the group. As soon as Maisy West had noticed his difficulty walking steadily, she had taken his hand and begun to lead him from child to child, making introductions. What an adult would have taken days to accomplish, Maisy had done in the space of an hour.

"I think we can leave now," Zoe said. "Go tell Patrick what we're doing so he won't worry."

Seeing his reticence, she laid a hand of comfort on his arm. "He will be fine here. Very safe. You know he needs the company of other children. They're not judging him the way adults might and he hasn't even looked at us for ages."

"Yeah. I see that."

Zoe stood back and watched her old friend approach the group of children, crouch and speak to his son as the others listened nearby. One of the boys spoke up, then Maisy followed with further assurances. By the time Sean stood, Patrick was already headed for a play area filled with large wooden blocks and obstacles.

"That gives me a great idea," Zoe told Sean as he returned to her. "We can run Angel through her paces in the training yard and encourage Patrick to do some of the exercises with her. The physical agility will undoubtedly help him."

To her chagrin, Sean scowled. "My son is not a dog."

She had to laugh. "No, but some of his best buddies are. Think of how encouraged he'll be if he can do what they do?"

"Such as?"

"Oh, I don't know. We won't ask him to climb, of course, but I imagine he'd love crawling through tunnels and under barricades." Enthusiasm for her brainchild grew until she wanted to clap her hands and jump for joy. "It's a wonderful idea. As a matter of fact, once Angel is certified as a therapy dog for you, you may want to continue training her and take her on visits to hospitals and rehab centers."

"Whoa. Hold on, lady. We haven't even taught her to stop jumping on me. Let's not get ahead of ourselves."

What she wanted to do was remind him that the Lord could accomplish anything, and that believers should always try their best, but she kept silent. He'd get there eventually. At least she hoped and prayed he would. If she looked back with honesty and candor, she could see how far Sean had already come. It would be wise to concentrate on that rather than focusing on how far he still had to go.

Whatever happened, she vowed to be there for him. How and when was unknown, yet nothing was impossible for God. Even if she had to quit her beloved Arizona job, she would. Hopefully it wouldn't come to that. Right now, her fondest wishes were a jumble of unknowns and confused thoughts, so she couldn't begin to decide what to ask or expect.

In her heart, she knew indecision was okay. No matter how much her mind argued, she would trust in her faith, in her Lord. All she really had to do was exercise patience.

That thought almost made her burst out laughing. There was a joke among believers about *never* praying for patience unless you wanted to be presented with long, long trials. Well, here she was, in the midst of just such a dilemma, with no end in sight. *Welcome to God's boot camp.*

She and Sean left the day care together and checked to be sure the dogs were comfortable in the car. Zoe slid behind the wheel while Sean got into the passenger seat. "Back to the training center?"

"Fine with me. I forgot to ask. Do they feed the kids lunch and snacks?"

"Yes. Are you hungry?" She pulled into traffic.

"I'm not sure. I feel kind of funny, as if I should

go back and get my son no matter how safe and happy he is. Does that make sense to you?"

"Of course. You're getting used to your new life, and he's a big part of it. You'll settle down more after you bond with Angel and the three of you become a team."

"I hope you're right."

Zoe chuckled softly. "Don't you know I'm always right, Murphy?"

"Yeah, well—"

Instant shattering of the side windows on her car interrupted him. Dual instincts made him duck and Zoe tromp the gas pedal to the floor.

She hadn't seen or sensed danger until it had been obvious. In order to have broken both windows simultaneously, a bullet must have passed from one side of the car to the other. Missing them both. *Praise God!* And thank Him that Patrick had not been present.

Eyes wide, head swiveling back and forth, Sean was bracing himself on the dashboard and shaking as if he'd been hit. "Where's the shooter?"

"I don't know," she shouted back. "Grab my phone and report it while I drive."

The desert air felt icy as it rushed through the broken windows. In the rear, the dogs barked, futilely warning intruders to stay away.

Zoe dodged through traffic and headed straight for the police station, hoping whoever had fired at them would be stupid enough to follow.

She slid into the open lot behind the station and jumped out to take up a defensive position behind the car door.

Sean circled the front of the vehicle to join her as cops raced out the back exit and surrounded them.

To her disappointment, whoever had shot at them had been smart enough to disappear. Chief Hayes tapped her on the shoulder and drew her away with Sean while others looked over the vehicle damage.

"We went back and rechecked that stolen red truck after we received the ballistics report I told you about. Most of the prints we lifted belonged to the teenagers we arrested, like I said, but there was one palm print that was unidentified. We ran that through AFIS. I have bad news for you."

"You got a match." Zoe wasn't asking. She knew.

"Yes," the chief said. "Whoever left that print has a record as long as your arm, including charges of homicide."

"So, the bullet in St. Louis is from an assassin's gun, and the print proves he or someone like him is here," she concluded.

"Afraid that's how it looks."

"Then how about putting a guard on Marilyn Carter's day care for us?" She was speaking to the chief but looking at Sean. "Sean's son Patrick isn't the only child who deserves protection. Your own daughter is there."

Hayes agreed. "Very sensible. What about you two?"

"I'll keep my guard up and so will Sean," Zoe said. "When we're not at my house, we'll be at the training center. It probably wouldn't hurt to keep a close eye on that, too."

"Will do." Chief Hayes offered his hand to Sean and they shook. "Don't hesitate to call if you even *think* you've seen something odd."

Before Zoe could explain for him, Sean spoke up. "I'm here because of a diagnosis of PTSD." He held out his trembling hands as a demonstration. "Are you *sure* you want me to call?"

The other man clapped him on the shoulder. "Absolutely. I'll tell you if it's too often. I don't want any more losses on my watch. Got that?"

"Yes, sir."

Sean's forceful agreement echoed his time in the military. So did his stiff posture. This was the first time Zoe had been privy to such a clear picture of his background. A lot had been imprinted. A lot would need to be mitigated because it could never be erased. He was the product of his past, as was she. They all were.

The secret to healing, as far as she could tell, was learning to face tragedy and figuring out how to find happiness despite whatever had happened.

Service dogs helped in some cases. Counseling and meds in others.

But she wanted more for Sean. She wanted him to have true peace and joy with his son by his side. To accomplish that, she and her fellow officers were going to have to do more than pat him on the back or give him a place to live or even find him the perfect canine companion.

They were going to have to end the reign of terror begun by the thugs who wanted to kill him. And then they were going to have to track down whoever had hired those men to keep it from recurring.

Given the enormity of that task, she didn't see any way to make it happen without calling upon divine intervention. Whether Sean believed or not, she was going to pray and keep praying. Fervently.

She was also going to stay armed. If God chose to work through her, she'd be ready.

SEVEN

The next few days kept Sean busy training with Angel. At night, when he took her home with him, she managed to settle down with Freya and avoid tearing up Zoe's house, much to his relief.

The progress Patrick had made was the most astounding of all. Sean wasn't sure whether to give the credit to Angel or Freya or the day care, particularly ten-year-old Maisy West. The few times he'd spotted her father in the distance and thought about praising the girl, however, the man hadn't looked approachable.

"Tell me about that guy, West," Sean said when he and Zoe were straightening up the kitchen after supper. "Why does he look mad at the world all the time?"

"Probably because he is." She sighed. "His wife was killed as the result of a home invasion. It's possible the perpetrators were after him, instead. I don't doubt he blames himself. I feel sorry for Maisy. She's kind of lost both parents at once."

"Well, she's sure been good for my son. I can't believe how well he's walking."

"Speaking of Patrick, where is he?"

Sean slipped the last slices of pizza onto a plate and refrigerated it. "Watching TV with the dogs while we do the dishes."

"Um, I don't think so."

"What do you mean? Of course he is. That's what they've done every evening."

She gestured with her chin since her hands were in soapy water. "Then where did she come from?"

Freya was peeking around the corner as if hoping he'd drop leftovers. There was no sign of Patrick.

Scowling, Sean ran past the dog so rapidly she edged her way to Zoe and sat at her feet, apparently waiting for orders.

"Did you find him?" Zoe was drying her hands when Sean returned.

"No. He's not in the living room or the hall or the bathroom."

"Well, he can't have gone far. Has he run off before?"

"Run?" Sean was incredulous. "He can hardly walk. How can he possibly be gone?"

"Calm down. We'll find him. He can't be far away."

Sean's trembling had returned, this time without flashbacks, and he raked his fingers through his short hair. "Not on his own, he can't. What if somebody kidnapped him?"

"With the dogs in the same room? Highly unlikely."

"Then what? Where is he?"

"I suspect he's using his newfound ability to walk better to explore the house. Let me get Freya's working harness on her and we'll do a professional search."

Sean knew he was being unreasonable but couldn't help shouting at her. "Why are you smiling?"

"Sorry," she said, although she continued to look pleased. "I'm just in my element right now. I'm not worried. I know the dog will track him down."

"Fine. You do this your way. I'm going to keep looking."

"If there is a scent trail, the less you muddle it, the better," Zoe said. "But suit yourself. You've both been all over the house, anyway." She held Freya's leash and straightened. "Wait a second. Where's Angel?"

"How should I know? She's always on the move." His scowl deepened, his fists clenching.

"There's a good chance she followed Patrick," Zoe said. "You stay here while I conduct my search."

"In a pig's eye. I'm coming with you."

"Why am I not surprised?" Pausing long enough

to lay a hand lightly on his forearm, she waited until his gaze met hers before she spoke. "Intense emotional reactions can affect everyone, including service dogs. I know it's hard for you to control your feelings. Everybody has trouble sometimes, particularly when a loved one is involved, but I'm going to ask you to really try this time. Take a deep breath and let it out slowly."

"You're wasting time."

"If I thought Patrick was in real danger, I'd already be on my way. Calm down and think rationally. The doors are locked. He can't have gotten out. And neither dog barked, so we know nobody broke in."

It took every ounce of Sean's strength to stand there and listen, to comprehend and consider that she might be right. Deep, slower breathing did help some. "All right. I'm as calm as I'm going to get. Can we go now?"

"Yes. Freya, find Patrick."

Tail wagging, tongue hanging out, the Belgian Tervuren looked up at her human partner as if asking for further instructions.

"Patrick." Zoe grabbed the boy's sweater off the back of the sofa and held it down for the dog to sniff. "Find."

Sean stepped aside as the pair passed. Zoe was not the only one who looked happy. The dog seemed just as pleased to be working. She entered the hallway, made several course adjustments, then headed for the room Zoe had given to her guests.

"I already looked in there," Sean insisted.

Zoe wasn't deterred. Neither was the K-9. She snuffled around the bed, then raised her head and made a beeline for the closet.

"They're in there," Zoe told Sean. "Open the door."

Ready to do battle because he didn't believe Patrick could have walked that far unassisted, he grasped the knob. Turned it. Heard muted giggling just as he jerked on the door, then froze. There they were. His son and Angel. Sitting on the closet floor and wrapped in the blanket they'd shared in the living room. Patrick's eyes were sparkling. The dog was alternately panting and licking the boy's cheeks as if agreeing that they had pulled off a great trick.

"How did you get in there?" Sean shouted.

Patrick's grin faded, and his eyes began to glisten. He not only lowered his head, he buried his face in the border collie's black-and-white ruff.

Sean immediately dropped to his knees. "I'm sorry, son. I didn't mean to scare you. I'm not mad. I was just so worried I yelled without thinking first." He opened his arms. "Come here."

Although the child moved slowly, he did go to Sean. So did Angel, which made the otherwise poignant moment more comedy than drama. Patrick had his arms around his daddy's neck, holding tightly. Angel was determined to kiss every face within reach.

Keeping one arm around his son, Sean looped the other over the dog's shoulders to help hold her still and avoid her wet tongue. Sort of. There was no way to keep her under full control, and, truth to tell, he didn't care if she showered him with doggy affection. She had not only followed his handicapped son, she had stayed with him despite the other dog's absence.

She might be too easily distracted as the trainers had reported, but she was loyal. And instinctively protective. No matter how hard he had to work to transform her into a good service dog, he was determined to succeed.

A shiver shot up his spine as his thoughts expanded on the premise. Would she be effective enough against enemies when her natural gift was for friendship? Should he ask for a more formidable-looking dog like a German shepherd or a Doberman, instead?

It didn't take long to reason that the likelihood of being assigned to a dog like that were slim and none. If Angel had not been available when he'd arrived at the training center, chances were he'd have been turned away. Therefore, she had been meant for him. For Patrick.

What he disliked most about that conclusion was the inference that a higher power may have arranged their pairing. Undoubtedly Zoe thought so. And perhaps the other trainers did, too. But that didn't mean he had to agree with them.

Trouble was, he was wondering if he might be wrong and they might be right. The fact that his enemies had driven him to Desert Valley, to the help he so desperately needed, was enough to upset his preconceived notions. Add to that the amazing assets that had awaited him here and you had a real conundrum.

Sean scooped up his son and carried him into the living room, where he settled with him on the sofa, pretending to watch TV while his mind sought answers that probably didn't exist.

Angel plopped down at his feet and rested her chin atop the toes of his shoes. All Sean said was, "Good girl."

Zoe gave man and boy a few moments alone before joining them. "Mind if I sit here, too?"

"Of course not."

She'd locked up her regular sidearm and was able to comfortably collapse next to them on the couch. "Long day."

"Yeah. Especially this last part."

Nothing could have kept her from smiling at the pair. "You should be thankful, you know."

"I know. It's just so unbelievable. A month ago he was barely able to stand. He was unresponsive for weeks before that."

"Kids are resilient. I understand the water

in the pool hadn't been heated. That was in his favor, too."

"So they tell me. The younger the child and the colder the water, the less lasting brain damage is done."

"Right." She produced a small electronic tablet and laid it in her lap. "I thought, if you're up to it, we could go over a few things. We need to figure out who is upset enough with you to want you dead."

"Beats me."

"Let's start with the families of the comrades in arms you visited after you returned to the States. Where did they live?"

"One was in Chicago. One was in Minneapolis. The other survivor had moved with no forwarding address. The folks in Chicago did talk to me, although they certainly didn't welcome me the way I'd hoped. It wasn't my fault the Humvee hit an IED. All I was trying to do was get to the airport so I could fly home to Patrick."

She saw his arms tighten around the drowsy child. "I could try to track down the soldier who moved as well as check on the backgrounds of the others if you like."

"Okay. Gentry was the family I couldn't find. Smiths were in Chicago. Yarnells were from Minneapolis. They were the ones who acted the most upset."

"I'll have Chief Hayes put out a few feelers and

see what he can come up with. How about your late wife's connections?"

"Those are a lot hazier. And far more likely to be with criminals. She was deeply involved in drugs."

"Do you know if there was an investigation after she overdosed? I'd think they'd at least look into identifying her supplier."

"So would I. Her parents, however, apparently pulled some strings to keep the whole thing hush-hush. No doubt they were embarrassed by Sandra's poor choices." He blew out a noisy sigh. "Including me as a husband."

Mulling over the information, or lack of it, Zoe finally asked, "Is it possible they just want control of Patrick?"

"Only an outside chance," Sean said flatly. "As I've said before, they could always sue for custody. I'm actually kind of surprised they haven't. Which reminds me, you and I haven't seen an attorney yet."

Her body moved imperceptibly as her mind retreated. "I think you should hold off on that. It's not that I don't want to help out, it's just that I suspect you'll find somebody special before long and build a new family. I don't want to stand in the way."

Waiting, barely breathing, she willed him to encourage her, at least by including her in the pool of eligible mates. He did not. Staring at the television, he acted as if he hadn't heard a word she'd said. Not speaking was more telling than denial. Silence told her that Sean was willing to view her as a buddy and accept her assistance in a pinch, yet not expand that image to include a lifelong commitment.

Okay. She got the picture. It hurt all the way from the roots of her dark brown hair to the tips of her toes, but she understood perfectly. They were friends, period.

That would do. It would have to.

Companionable stillness enveloped Sean. Patrick had fallen asleep in his lap, so he had no qualms about bringing up Christmas plans. Anything but face the touchy subject Zoe had tried to discuss.

"Do you want me to get a tree and ornaments, or will it create too much excitement for the dogs?" he asked.

"I've given that some thought. I'll pick up a small one and put it on the table in the kitchen. That way they'll know it's off-limits." She sighed. "What about presents for you-know-who? I have no idea what to buy him."

"You don't have to give him anything."

"I want to. He's a real sweetheart. Why wouldn't I give him something for Christmas?"

"I just don't want you to feel obligated."

"In that case, I'll cross you off my list. Patrick is getting presents."

"Okay, okay. Don't get huffy."

"*Huffy?* You want to see huffy, you just try to stop me from making this the best Christmas he's ever had."

Sean partially let go of the boy in order to raise one hand in surrender. What in the world was wrong with Zoe? She was usually so even-tempered and levelheaded. "No argument here," he said. "I was just trying to make things easier for you."

"I love Christmas, okay? If I were home in Mesa, I'd have my whole apartment decorated, even the cactus in front of my picture window. I do it every year."

"And instead, you're stuck here with us."

"I'm not stuck anywhere, Murphy. I'm here because I choose to be, and you're staying in my house by my invitation, so don't go imagining me as some suffering martyr. I'll buy some decorations that I can easily take home afterward. You can pick up anything else you want. It makes no difference to me."

Eyeing her and sensing continued animosity, he decided it was best to merely nod. He'd never been big on a lot of tinsel and colored lights. Hadn't even had a tree since childhood. Sandra's parents, Alice and John Shepherd, had always gone overboard on fancy decorations, and she had dragged him to their house whenever he was home on leave around holiday time. They hadn't done all the work themselves, of course, and the result had always been so perfect he'd found it off-putting.

Finally he ventured a comment. "Do you think we could talk a couple of your police friends into shopping with us? I'd feel safer if others were along."

Zoe nodded and arched an eyebrow. "That's a good idea. I'll ask Dalton or Tristan if they're available."

"I know about West. Who did you say the other guy was?"

"A former soldier who recently married one of the local school teachers. He's been raising his teenage niece, too. You and he have more in common than some of the others."

"Have you told him about me?"

It surprised him to hear her say, "No." The reasons were even more impressive. "I hadn't asked you if I could share your story with anybody except the dog trainers, so I didn't. If you want to make it public, that's up to you."

He knew he was staring when she said, "What?"

"Nothing. I just figured the whole town knew by now."

"Gossip can spread fast in a close-knit community, but they didn't learn any secrets from me."

"Thank you."

"You're welcome." Zoe got to her feet and

stretched, arms over her head. "Turn off the lights when you decide to go to bed."

"Good night." Sean wanted to say so much more. To tell her what she'd meant to him, now and in the past. To compliment her on her expertise and choosing a career of service. To thank her again and again for opening her home to him and her heart to his son.

His cheeks warmed when he pictured himself thanking Zoe with a hug as she left him. Instead, he gently eased the boy off his lap and laid him on the couch, then made the rounds of windows and doors, rechecking the locks before doing it all a second time. Yes, he was paranoid. That was only crazy if nobody was after him. He knew the danger remained, just as he knew his nerves were balanced on a knife-edge between self-control and sheer panic.

Every time he peered out into the darkness, he thought undefined objects moved. Shifted. Inched closer. Then he'd blink and the supposed danger would vanish.

He flicked off the kitchen lights and paused at the window over the sink. Moonlight cast parts of the yard in darkness while gleaming off bare rocks and crags in the distance.

A shiver shot up his spine. Instinct pushed him back into the interior shadows. Held him there. Made him wonder if his mind was playing tricks as it often did.

Then he saw a pattern of light and dark pass across the bare floor. It lingered only for a second. Was this for real? Was someone watching? Waiting for him to make a mistake?

Edging closer to the window frame, Sean held his breath and continued to scan the yard for intruders. Nothing presented itself, not even a passing nocturnal animal.

He left all the interior lights off to keep from highlighting himself, then once again made the rounds of all the windows. His musings progressed from a heightened sense of danger to an assurance that his damaged mind had been responsible for the fright.

"All right," he mumbled, sighing. "So there was nothing there this time." That didn't matter. He was not about to let down his guard. Not if folks called him crazy for the rest of his life. Which, hopefully, would be a good long time.

EIGHT

Sunday morning came early for Zoe. Even Freya seemed inclined to sleep in—until Angel nosed open the door and came barreling into the room, caromed off the edge of the bed and sped back out. If her barking had not been so high-pitched and playful, Zoe would have worried.

Instead of reaching for her sidearm, she stretched and yawned. Freya did the same. This was a special day. A morning filled with promise and possibilities.

A silly notion made her smile and mutter, "Yes, as long as nobody tries to shoot us." That attitude made her shake her head at herself. How could she hope to convince Sean to trust God if she went around making jokes about divine intervention? Then again, humor was good medicine. The Bible said so.

By the time she'd dressed, the aroma of freshly brewed coffee and sizzling bacon had drifted down the hall. There was a lot to be said for a guy who pitched in and cooked.

She breezed into the kitchen, smiling. "Wow. Something smells great!"

Judging by the way Sean stopped moving and stared, she'd either made a good impression or a very bad one. She whirled, arms out. "What do you think? I love this red sweater."

"It's—it's pretty."

A slight blush accentuated his approval and appreciation of her efforts. She seldom wore more than lipstick, but this morning had splurged using eyebrow pencil and a touch of eye shadow. Gold hoop earrings replaced the plain gold studs she wore while training and working.

"Thanks. I didn't bring a skirt from home, but at least I'm not wearing jeans."

"I don't have fancy clothes," Sean said, looking down at his jeans and boots. "Maybe I should just stay here."

"Not on your life." Zoe grinned. "I figure, if a church doesn't accept people for who they are instead of what they wear or how much money is in their wallets, then they shouldn't bother opening their doors."

"I have to warn you, I'm not comfortable in crowds."

"We can sit all the way to the rear, with our backs against the wall. Will that help?"

"Hopefully. Just don't be surprised if I have to take a break during the service."

That's fine. We'll include Freya for moral support."

"Not Angel?"

She wanted to jump for joy. "If you want her with us, that's fine. The Community Church is used to handlers bringing their dogs. Nobody will think it's odd."

"That's a relief. I was afraid I'd stand out."

Zoe wanted to comment that he'd stand out simply because he was so attractive, despite his often somber mood, but she refrained. The less attention they called to themselves, the better. Plus, there would be plenty of police officers at the morning service, both in the sanctuary and posted in the hallways, just in case of trouble from outsiders. Therefore, she saw no need to strap on her duty weapon or tuck a spare gun at her waist and spoil the way her red pullover fit.

"Okay." Zoe took a place at the table next to Patrick. "Let's eat so we can get this show on the road. Right, kiddo?"

The child paused and inclined his head for a moment before he said, "At-rick."

Sean whipped around. His jaw gaped. "Patrick?"

Pressing her lips together and leaning closer, Zoe made the sound for *P*, then followed it with the rest of his name. She thought she and Sean were both going to cry when the little boy echoed, "P-atrick."

Because of the broken windows in Zoe's car, they took Sean's pickup to church. The parking lot was far more crowded than Sean had expected. He chose a spot on the fringes.

Sean recognized Dalton West because he was with Maisy. Patrick spotted her and led the way to the pair by tugging on his daddy's hand and leaning.

"Your daughter has made quite an impression on my son in day care," Sean said, trying to keep Angel from jumping all over the children and licking their faces.

"New dog?" Dalton eyed the border collie.

"Very new. So am I. She's supposed to help me with PTSD."

"I can tell that from her vest." Dalton shot a concerned look toward Zoe, then said, "May I?" and reached for Angel's leash.

"Sure," Sean said. "She's settled down a lot at home but still gets really excited in new situations."

Instead of answering, Dalton faced the dog, pointed a finger at her, then quickly brought it to his own face. "Look at me. Look. Sit."

She not only obeyed the calm, firm instructions, she sat still at West's feet and kept staring into his eyes. He didn't babble or keep repeating her name, nor did he make unnecessary motions. He merely exuded authority.

Sean was flabbergasted. "Wow. What did you do to my crazy dog?"

"Took command," the other man said as he passed the end of the leash back to Sean. "You can learn to do it, too. It just takes time."

"Thanks for the lesson." Eyeing the children, Sean asked about Sunday school.

"Maisy usually sits in church with me," Dalton said.

The dark-haired ten-year-old tugged at her father's hand. "I can take Patrick to the kindergarten class and stay with him today, can't I? Please?"

"If it's okay with Mr. Murphy."

"I'll— We'll walk with you," Sean said. "Lead the way." A backward glance at Zoe made Sean wish she were by his side. No. Zoe was too wonderful. She needed a man who was perfect, not an emotionally wounded one like himself. She deserved better. He just wished...

What? What did he wish? That he had been wiser as a younger man? That he had realized how ideal Zoe was when they were college students? That he had waited to marry? His imagination paused before adding, *That Patrick was her son.* Hers and his. And that she'd be the one to help raise him.

Entering the church with the others, Sean

hardly noticed where he was. Someone tried to hand him a bulletin. Angel promptly accepted it for him, gave it a shake, then carried it as she trotted obediently at his side.

Short hair at Sean's nape began to prickle. He fought off the sensation. It kept building. If he had been sitting down, he knew he would have had to get up and move. To flee his invisible enemies.

Zoe touched his arm. "Are you all right?"

"No. It's claustrophobic in here."

"Okay. I'll finish escorting Patrick to class. You can wait for me outside."

"He'll be scared without me."

"It'll be worse if you suddenly have a flashback and he has to watch," she said tenderly. "Go. If anybody asks, tell them the dog needed to go out. That way you won't be embarrassed. I'll join you in a few minutes."

"If you have any trouble, bring Patrick back to me. Promise?"

"I promise."

Turning on his heel, Sean headed for the exit. Angel gave him no argument, sticking to his side as if she'd suddenly realized he needed her. Perhaps she had. Whatever the reason, he was relieved to not have to drag her or fight to keep her from jumping on others.

The glass door swung open. Sean was barely able to hesitate long enough to permit a couple with small children to enter before he sidled past them with his dog and burst out into the open. His heart was pounding, his breath shallow and quick. One stride. Two. Then more, until he reached a place where he could be alone enough to regain his composure.

Exhausted, he leaned against the side of his pickup bed and forced himself to inhale deeply, slowly. He'd almost waited too long. Almost embarrassed Zoe in front of her friends. Instincts for self-preservation were supposed to keep a person out of trouble, not cause it, and his were clearly wide of the mark.

Watching for Zoe and Freya, Sean reached down and laid his hand on Angel's soft fur. Stroking her head seemed to calm him, and when she tried to give him the soggy church bulletin he almost smiled. "Yes, you're a good girl. It would be nice if both of us weren't wonky but you're coming along well. I guess we will work out."

The glass side door reflected sunshine and vehicles as it swung open again. Sean started to straighten before he realized it wasn't Zoe passing through. He relaxed and looked away. Then his head snapped around. He'd almost failed to recognize the beefy hit man wearing Sunday clothing. And there was a telltale bulge under the arm of his sports jacket to confirm that he was armed.

Sean eased around the pickup and kept his head down as he watched the would-be assailant. A uniformed officer of the DVPD had followed him outside and was resting his palm on the butt of his sidearm while calling, "Wait!"

If the hit man replied, Sean didn't hear it. He didn't have to. He saw enough. The man hailed a dark SUV and climbed inside, leaving the cop standing alone in the lot.

It was impossible to ID the driver due to darkly tinted windows. When the vehicle accelerated out of the parking lot, Sean expelled his breath in a whoosh. They were gone. For now.

As he started to stand, his innate wariness kicked in again and he muttered, "Assuming there are only those two."

Zoe had trouble spotting Sean so she commanded Freya to find Angel. That was all it took.

She hurried up and greeted him with a smile in spite of his frown. "The kids are all set. Are you ready to go back inside?"

"I'm not sure. Not after what I just saw."

Waiting, she raised an eyebrow. When he failed to volunteer information, she asked. "What did you see?"

"One of the guys who came to Arizona after me."

A frisson of fear shot up her spine as she wheeled to face the church. "Where? When?"

"He came out and got into a black SUV with a second man. They drove away in spite of one of the cops calling to him."

"When?"

"Just now."

"You're sure it was the same guy?" She hated to question Sean's judgment, but his record of being correct was less than perfect. He was, however, apparently ultrasensitive to danger. The key was learning to differentiate between the real thing and figments of his imagination.

"As sure as I can be under these circumstances," Sean said dryly. "Being paranoid doesn't mean there's nobody after me. Your car did get shot up."

"True." Continuing to scan their surroundings, Zoe kept Freya at heel. "You're sure you saw them leave?"

"Yes. I don't know why they were here in the first place. I mean, if they wanted to harm me, why not shoot when I came out here?"

"Maybe they didn't see you leave."

"It's more likely that," Sean agreed. "I wouldn't want to cause trouble in a church full of cops."

"So, you're ready to come back in with me?"

"I have to. Patrick is in there."

"Right," she said. "I'll alert church security to watch for the SUV, just in case. We can find seats in the rear of the sanctuary and sneak out just before the altar call so we're waiting when his class dismisses."

Although Sean agreed by not arguing, she could tell he was far from settled. As before, she would take one moment at a time, ready for intervention if necessary yet hopeful that his troubled mind would allow him to actually benefit from the pastor's sermon. Beyond that, she had no plans.

"Freya, heel," she said, stepping out to lead the way. Was Sean following? She wanted to look back to be certain. Instead, she kept walking until they reached side windows on the building where she could see their reflections. Her pulse jumped. Sean's posture looked good. Straight, tall and in command. Was wishful thinking influencing her, or he had actually made some progress? That didn't matter as much as the fact that he was functioning well despite his recent scare.

When she'd first spoken with him about coming to Desert Valley, he had not seemed nearly as sure of himself or able to cope. Research had told her that his traumatic past might always color his future, but she also knew that some degree of healing was possible. *With God, all things are possible.*

If she had ever doubted that biblical truth, she didn't anymore. Truth to tell, nobody but God was in charge of their future.

All Zoe prayed for at this point was her friend's happiness and well-being. If Sean's life was to include her, she would be overjoyed. If not, she would somehow accept that, too. She either trusted her heavenly Father in all things, including the long-ago loss of her ill, helpless baby brother, or she didn't.

For years she'd assumed that childhood disappointment had cost her the most dearly of any. Now, realizing how much she cared for Sean and his son, she knew better. Losing him, for any reason, was going to hurt so much she might never recover. The mere thought was enough to tie her stomach in knots and make her wish she had skipped breakfast.

He touched her elbow. "Are you all right?"

A shiver zinged up her spine and tickled the back of her neck.

"Of course. Why?" Their eyes met in the mirrorlike window glass. His body language spoke of protection. His height and strength giving her an instant sense of awareness that made her insides quake.

"You seemed different," he snorted. "Don't tell me *that* was all in my head, too."

"No." She turned to look directly at him and tried to smile. Their lips were so close, the idea of initiating a kiss so tempting, she swayed, fighting to keep from leaning toward him. Suppose he was resistant? Suppose he wasn't as enamored of her as she hoped? Suppose she ruined their close friendship by taking it to a new level before he was ready?

Zoe sighed. "I was thinking too much, that's all."

"About me?"

What could she say that would be the truth,

yet not reveal her burgeoning love for man and boy? Imagining his tender kiss was already bad enough, so she turned his question into a gibe. "If I say yes, will you get all sappy on me?"

Sean gave a wry chuckle. "I think you're safe. I'm too busy trying to keep this dog in line and make sure nobody is trying to sneak up and shoot me while I'm distracted. I don't have room in my brain for excess sentimentality."

Although she said, "That's a relief," she was disappointed. Her brain certainly had enough room to entertain romantic notions while still doing her job.

"Well, this threat can't last forever," Sean said, adding, "I hope."

In Zoe's mind a worst-case scenario began to form. If they didn't manage to nab the thugs or figure out who had sent them in the first place, the only other way this story was all going to end was if Sean was killed. There had to be a different answer. Anything was better than that.

Witness protection was out because Sean didn't qualify. And he certainly couldn't go back into the military. Not with PTSD. Neither could he join her profession. Besides, if he wasn't around anymore, who would look after his little boy?

That brought her back to their verbal agreement about custody.

Zoe sighed as she started into the main sanctuary and led the way to seats in the rear for Sean's sake. The more she was with him, the greater her affection grew. Did he suspect how she felt? Was it possible he was falling for her, too?

The shake of her head was barely perceptible. If Sean cared for her, he would be sending out clues, and she wasn't getting any hints at all. Perhaps it was time to quit hoping their pact about Patrick's care would be fulfilled by a mutual love and take the legal steps they had discussed in the beginning. The drawback was that that might satisfy Sean and keep him from considering alternatives.

Such as marriage.

NINE

Maisy not only led a giggling Patrick into the hall outside his classroom after church, she also made a convincing speech about the benefits of letting the boy participate in the children's Christmas pageant.

"He can be a shepherd," she insisted when Sean began to slowly shake his head. "He'd get a cane to lean on and everything. And I'll be right there." She began to beam. "I'm playing Mary."

"How much time would he have to practice with all the others?" Sean asked. "It might take him a while to catch on."

"We'll all help him." The tenderhearted child took Patrick's hand. "He can do it. Please, please, please?"

Sean was about to make more excuses when Patrick smiled up at him and said, "Peas?"

What could he do or say at that point? "All right. What about practicing? When do you do that?"

"Tonight during church for grown-ups," Maisy said. "My dad helps. So does Chief Hayes."

Zoe was agreeing. "That's right. And I can be there, too, if you're worried. Sophie's acting the part of one of the Magi with the chief's daughter, Lily, and a couple of dogs. It should be worth watching just to see a Labrador retriever pretending to be a camel."

As far as Sean was concerned, the added exposure was foolish. However, he could also see how much progress toward normalcy Patrick had made since being allowed his freedom among a group of helpful children. Maisy, alone, was a godsend.

That conclusion brought him up short, particularly the definition his subconscious had chosen. To imagine that God had sent anything his way seemed odd. Still, anyone who was privy to the events that had brought him and his son to Desert Valley had to be thinking the same thing. A happy coincidence was one, maybe two, actions that were of benefit. He was seeing dozens, from the original accident to Patrick all the way to this very moment. Along the way, a myriad of connections had been made and people were in places where they would not normally have been. Take Zoe. She should have been at work in Mesa, yet here she was, just where and when he needed her.

Stunned, he had to admit that there may have

been a divine hand guiding him to Desert Valley. Many questions remained, though. Such as, why did the boy have to suffer and why was his own mind affected adversely—and why was somebody so determined to harm him?

Sean blinked rapidly to clear his head and realized he was standing in a crowded hallway with all sorts of people milling around and pushing past, laughing and talking. It was too much. An assassin could be right next to him, and he wouldn't know until it was too late.

He looked at Zoe. "We need to go."

"I see that. Give me Angel's leash and bring Patrick." She started to steer both dogs toward the closest exit.

"The truck's on the other side of the church," Sean reminded her.

"I know. I thought it would be best to get outside ASAP and then circle around. Besides, the dogs need room to move, to stretch their legs."

And so do I. Sean inhaled deeply, trying to force a calm he wasn't feeling. They broke into the sunlight, and the warmth on his face bathed him in peace. When the time came for him to look for employment, finding work outside was probably going to be best.

"Assuming I can keep it together long enough to look for a job," he muttered, half disgusted with himself even though he knew his brain had been affected by a trauma he could not have anticipated or avoided.

Zoe overheard him. "You're thinking about a job? Good for you. That's a step in the right direction."

"Yeah. All I have to do is add a dog to my résumé."

"Stranger things have happened." She paused and shaded her eyes. "I think you're doing very well."

"What about the incident in the parking lot before church started?"

"That's only a bad thing if it was all in your head. You're still sure you recognized the guy?"

"Oh, yeah. It was him all right."

"Then stop beating yourself up about it. The only thing you can really influence is your own actions. We'll face the rest when and if it happens."

"If?" His eyebrows arched. "You act like you think my problems are just going to vanish. Well, they're not. I'm a basket case, my son is half the kid he once was and I'm in more personal danger than I was overseas."

"I don't know that I'd go that far," she countered. "Here, you have the whole police force—and me—on your side."

"And by being here I'm putting you in jeopardy," Sean said. He'd have reached for her hands if she hadn't been holding both leashes and he hadn't had hold of Patrick.

Instead of acting the way he'd expected, Zoe smiled. "There is no place you could possibly be that would be better for self-defense than this town. And there is no better lookout than a dog. Your senses may not be up to par, but Angel's are. Stop borrowing trouble. This will all work out for the best."

"How can you believe that?"

"Because I've seen it happening all around me, ever since I became a Christian," she said. "You'd see it too if you'd just open your eyes and your mind."

"What about the bullet that took out your car windows?"

Laughter bubbled, leaving Sean astounded, particularly when she said, "It missed *us*, didn't it?"

Evening church was a more casual gathering, and although there was a short sermon, Zoe didn't mind skipping it in order to accompany Patrick and his father to the rehearsal for the Christmas pageant.

They gathered with the children and an assortment of dogs in the fellowship hall. Although the simple drama was to be staged outside under special lighting and with background music, rehearsals were handled inside.

She stood back as one of the volunteers fitted Patrick and several other boys with brownish robes and head coverings. Sean had accompanied them into the large hall that was half meeting room and half gymnasium, depending upon the current need. Children's chattering and laughter filled the space.

Zoe leaned toward Sean. "So far, so good?"

"I'll live. I think."

"That makes one of us." Grinning, she looped Freya's leash over her wrist and covered her ears with both hands. "I don't know why schoolteachers don't have headaches all the time."

"Maybe they do. I wish Patrick had had more time to learn what to do."

Zoe wasn't worried. "Don't sweat the small stuff. It looks as though Maisy has arranged for the newest shepherd to be shepherded by at least two others. Look, they're even sharing their crooks. He'll be fine."

"He does seem happy."

"And that's what matters," Zoe reminded him. "This is for Patrick more than us." Realizing that she had inadvertently joined herself with Sean as a couple, she blushed and hoped he hadn't noticed.

There was no denying how she felt. If she had been around the boy from the time he was a baby, she didn't think she would love him more than she already did. *And his daddy? Oh, yes.* No matter where Sean went or how much he did or did not recover, she loved him dearly.

In her deepest heart, she knew she always had.

* * *

Supervisors moved the children outside as soon as the Sunday-school director announced, "We have time for one run-through with the manger."

Sean kept his eye on his son and followed closely. So did Zoe. Angel wasn't behaving as well as Freya, but she'd quit straining at the leash and trying to kiss every kid she saw. As far as he was concerned, that was a big breakthrough.

He touched Zoe's arm. "I don't like moving them outside."

"You know we have security on duty whenever church is in session. Besides, nobody knew we were going to be staging on-site tonight. The actual dress rehearsal was set for Tuesday night with performances on Wednesday and Friday evenings."

Sean didn't hide his concern. "I hadn't considered that much exposure. Maybe I should pull Patrick out."

"Don't you dare. He's going to have this wonderful experience if I have to hog-tie you to keep you out of it."

"Hey, tell me what you really think." He managed a smile for her benefit. "Okay. But one sign of trouble, and we're out of here."

"What could possibly happen in a group of great people like these? Look how the boys his age are helping him find his place and sharing the shepherds' crooks."

"I see." Sean sighed. Zoe was probably right. She had been so far. It was just that his skin kept crawling, and the hair at his nape prickled with warnings. Yes, he was not normal. And, yes, the church people had been great to accept him and his son. Yet there remained a sense of uneasiness that refused to go away no matter how much assurance he got.

The children assembled, ready to march up to the manger beneath the makeshift shelter. Mary and Joseph sat beside each other, gazing fondly at the baby doll, while older girls dressed as angels with impressive white wings sang along with recorded Christmas carols playing loudly in the background.

It was time for the shepherds' entrance. Sean could see the crooks sticking up above the costumed heads of the children. From where he stood it was hard to pick out Patrick, so he looked for a halting gait, instead. None stood out.

Sean scowled. Shaded his eyes against the floodlights illuminating the tableau. One, two, three, four… He grabbed Zoe's wrist. "How many shepherds are there supposed to be?"

"Five?"

"That's what I thought." He shoved Angel's leash at her and shouldered closer to the costumed boys. There were exactly four dressed as shepherds.

His son was not one of them!

"Patrick!"

* * *

Zoe would have beaten Sean to the front if she hadn't had to manage both dogs. Even Freya was acting out. Little wonder, with Angel leaping against the constraints of her harness and making a terrible racket, half barking, half whining and howling.

"Maisy," Zoe called over the swell of the music, "do you see Patrick?"

The girl stood. Looked into the background. Shook her head—and immediately abandoned her part as Mary to press in among the younger children.

After that, pandemonium reigned. Joseph was yelling at her to come back. Shepherds milled around, unsure whether or not to follow Mary, and the Magi broke ranks, with Sophie and Ryder's old dog, Titus, in the lead.

Sophie shouted to Zoe. "Circle to the left. I'll take the right with my dog. Everybody else freeze."

Without question, teachers rounded up the children and kept them in a tight group around the staging.

Passing through, Sean was yanking the head coverings off any child who even slightly resembled his son. Zoe could tell he hadn't found Patrick because he kept going until he had removed them all.

She joined him, facing the parking lot. Beyond lay a stand of ponderosa pines surrounded by rocks and dust and uninhabited desert. Was it possible the little boy had gotten that far? If so, he was liable to be stunned by the cold the winter night brought, not to mention the possibility of a slight snowfall. Thankfully, all the children had been costumed over their jackets and sweaters, but that didn't mean Patrick would stay warm all night.

Sean's blue eyes sparked with anger. And fear. "Where is he?"

"He's probably just playing hide-and-seek the way he did when he hid in the closet. We'll find him." She believed they would. They must. The only real worry was how long it might take.

Sophie came up with Titus and began stripping the old yellow Lab of his costume. "I've called the station and requested more dogs and handlers. Until they get here, I'm going to start Titus. He's not the tracker he used to be, but there was none as good when he was younger."

She looked at Zoe and Sean. "Do either of you have anything of the boy's? A scarf, hat, glove? Anything?"

Sean reached into his jacket pocket. "He took his gloves off when they put his costume on him."

"Perfect." Snatching the small, padded mittens, Sophie presented them to the old dog, let him sniff for a few seconds, then said, "Find."

Knowing what to expect gave Zoe comfort.

Unfortunately, that did not transfer to Sean. He started to follow Titus.

Zoe grabbed a handful of his jacket. "No. Let them work. If you interfere, you'll confuse the dog."

Anger flashed from his eyes. His body was so obviously tense, so primed for action, she was surprised her efforts even slowed him down.

She'd looped the ends of both leashes over her wrist to free her hands and used both on his arm to hold him back. "Stop. Think. That dog is trained and you're not. Let him work." As his focus shifted to her she added, "Please?"

"I'll give you to the count of ten, then I'm going. Understand? Patrick could barely walk a week ago. There's no way he got far on his own."

"I know. I agree, up to a point. But he's been doing so well since Maisy started encouraging him, I think you may underestimate his abilities."

A shout came from the dimness. Dogs barked. Zoe's heart jumped along with her body. Releasing her hold on Sean, she started to run toward the sound, and in the process lost hold of Angel.

Freya paced Zoe while Sean and the border collie raced ahead. It was easy to keep Angel in sight due to the bright white parts of her coat. Zoe could have cheered and wept at the same time when she saw the dog stop and circle.

They'd found Patrick. It had to be him. It just had to be. *Please, God, let him be all right.*

Sean was on his knees by the time she got to him. His arms were wrapped around his son, his face buried on the child's shoulder. Angel kept circling, and Titus was barking, proudly announcing news of his success.

A sobbing Maisy tugged on Zoe's jacket. "It's—it's all my fault. I told him I'd help him go get another crook for the boy who gave him his. Only I meant later. Will my daddy be mad at me?"

"I'll explain for you," Zoe assured her. She looked at Sean and noticed how tense he appeared. "Relax. We found him. No harm done."

"That's what you think." Gesturing at several uniformed officers and their K-9 partners who were disappearing into the shadows of the trees, he said, "Patrick didn't walk all the way out here by himself. He says a strange man promised to help him find a long stick and carried him this far."

"What man?"

"Exactly. I strongly doubt it was a member of the church. That leaves only one other option."

"Impossible," Zoe insisted. "If kidnappers had taken him, they'd still have him. They wouldn't have let him go."

"That was my first thought—until he told me somebody else told the man to put him down and wait for me."

"Wait for you? Did he say why?" There was no

real reason to ask that question, but Zoe had to hear for herself.

Sean's eyebrows arched. "Why do you think? They'd probably still be waiting here to ambush me if the police response hadn't been so overwhelming and fast. And if there hadn't been dogs in the lead."

He stared into the woods where the officers and other working K-9s had disappeared in pursuit. Patrick was hugging his daddy and acting as insecure as he had when Zoe had first met him. Poor kid. *He gets a little independence back, starts to enjoy it and his whole world falls apart.*

Finally, Zoe held out her hand to the boy. "Come with me, Patrick. We need to go back to rehearsal."

"No way." Sean cupped the boy's tousled head. "He's through standing around outside where I can't hold on to him."

"Whoever bothered him is long gone with half the DVPD on their heels. There's no place safer than the church right now."

"I said, no."

There was enough ire in Sean's voice to have made a grown man quail, so Zoe wasn't surprised that the little boy began to sniffle and cry.

She stood as tall as her slim frame would allow and tried to appear formidable. "I understand your concern, but stop and think about it. If everything you say is true, then it's you who needs to stay out of sight, not your little boy." Signaling with a nod toward the church she added, "Move, before I have you handcuffed and put in protective custody for your own good."

"You wouldn't dare."

Facing him with every ounce of courage she possessed, Zoe managed to sound convincing when she said, "I will do anything I need to in order to keep you safe, Murphy. Even make you mad at me, if that's what it takes."

A shout from the woods and intense barking brought Sean up short in the church parking lot. He looked to Zoe. "Hear that?"

"Yes. It sounds as though they caught him."

"I almost hate to get my hopes up."

Ellen Foxcroft joined them, waving a radio and grinning. "Did you hear?"

"Hear what?"

"They got the guy. And he's the one who left the palm print on the stolen truck!"

They're sure?" Sean asked.

"Positive ID."

Mirroring the other K-9 officer's grin, Zoe glanced at Sean. "See? I told you this police force was good."

"What about the second man?" Sean asked. "Did they spot him, too?"

Ellen sobered. "Not yet. We're close. As soon

as the suspect in custody talks, we'll pick him up, too."

"Was this guy driving a black SUV?"

"Yes. They're dusting it for fingerprints now. Should have AFIS results on any partners he may have had before the end of the night."

Zoe whispered, "Thank You, Jesus."

Sean swallowed hard. He was almost ready to agree.

TEN

Sean went back to training Angel with Ellen and Sophie the following week, trusting his son to the day care. Now that they were aware of Patrick's improved mobility, everybody would be taking more precautions. He actually felt sorry for ten-year-old Maisy West. She'd taken a personal interest in helping Patrick and therefore blamed herself for his mistakes.

After careful consideration, Sean had come to the conclusion that Maisy's tender mothering had helped the boy a lot more than anything and anybody else had, including himself. He and Dalton, her father, were in similar circumstances. Both children lacked a parent. Perhaps Maisy needed Patrick as much as he needed her.

And what do I need? Sean asked himself. A lovely image appeared in his mind. It was Zoe, of course. Who else would it be? He could picture her fitting into many areas of his life, including becoming Patrick's mother. She'd be good at it. If he weren't so imperfect, he might even seriously consider asking her to marry him.

For Patrick's sake? Sure. Partly. But there was another reason, one that kept needling him, awake or asleep. He didn't want to be separated from his dear friend ever again. *Because?* Because, like it or not, he was in love with her.

Patrick made it through the second dress rehearsal without a glitch. To the boy's credit, he didn't seem at all nervous when Wednesday night arrived. Happily, someone had come up with a fifth shepherd's crook, so each little actor was similarly equipped.

Angel went everywhere with Sean, as per instructions, and had settled into her job with amazing ease. No matter how relaxed and calm she seemed to be, her ears were always perked, her eyes keeping watch. For Sean, it was like being surrounded by a cadre of alert bodyguards. Nobody was going to sneak up on him—or his son— with Angel on duty.

The change in his outlook had occurred quickly, and although he knew anything could still upset his peace, he felt 100 percent better. So good, in fact, that he didn't stop himself when he got the urge to hold Zoe's hand while they watched the pageant performance.

As her fingers slipped between his, a sense of rightness flowed over and through him. Not only had she failed to object, she was returning the affectionate gesture.

Her shoulder bumped his. "Look. Here they come."

"I see. All five of them, thankfully."

"Exactly. Thanks to the good Lord, all is well and getting better. Right?"

Sean shrugged a little. "Okay. I'll give you that. And thanks to the Desert Valley police, one of my assailants is off the streets. Any word on the other guy?"

"Not yet. He may have hit the road when his buddy was picked up. He's not exactly able-bodied with one arm in a cast."

"Unless he's ambidextrous, it's his gun hand, too."

"True. Is that why you seem so much better?"

"That, and the dog," Sean said. "Having Angel with me makes a lot more difference than I'd thought it would. All she really has to do is be there and keep watch. Now that she's used to me and Patrick, she's taking her job very seriously."

"As she should." Zoe leaned on him, shoulder to shoulder, and squeezed his hand. "Aren't the kids cute? Look at that angel in the back. She keeps yawning and knocking her tinsel halo crooked."

"Here comes the hero dog, or should I say camel. I can't imagine why they'd retire a great dog like Titus."

"Arthritis and stamina, mostly," Zoe said.

"Chief Hayes took him home to be a pet for Lily. His new dog, Phoenix, knocked over their Christmas tree but Titus is a good boy."

"That reminds me. We never shopped for the decorations I promised you."

"One project at a time," Zoe whispered. "The most important thing is getting you and your dog squared away and making sure that last suspect is captured. Then we'll shop or hike or whatever you want. I still have a couple of weeks left on my lease. We may as well enjoy the desert while we can." She shivered. "Even if it does get cold after dark."

The Magi with their canine camels filed in, led by Titus and Sophie and followed by another yellow Lab who didn't act nearly as complacent about having extra gear strapped to his back. Zoe giggled. "That's Tristan McKeller's dog, Jesse. He's a lot younger than Titus."

"Aren't there supposed to be three wise men?"

"There are. Maybe the third camel had to go on duty and miss this performance."

"I'll sure be glad when all this stuff is over." Sean gave her fingers a gentle press. "I know it's good for Patrick but..."

"I do understand. The thing is, you can't expect him to make progress if you continue to baby him. We've seen great results in the few weeks you've been here."

He made a face. "Yeah. I don't like admitting it, but you're right."

"Of course I am. Humble, too."

Muted chuckles apparently made Angel look up at Sean. He didn't react to her movements until she stood and bristled. Could she be jealous of his feelings for Zoe?

"The dog," Zoe said. "Look at your dog."

"I see her. What do you think is wrong?"

"I don't know." She gathered Freya on a tight leash and scanned the crowd. "You stay here and keep an eye on Patrick. I'm going to circle around to the back of the set and investigate."

"He's fine," Sean said.

Only when he looked again, he didn't see his son. Four crooks stood tall in the rear of the tableau. The fifth was gone.

Zoe was already on her way when she heard Sean shout, "Patrick!" Nobody had to explain. Panic was so evident in the man's voice she knew the child was out of sight. The question was, where had he gone this time? Had the second thug taken him despite all their precautions? That seemed impossible. Patrick had been warned about strangers, so he wouldn't have willingly submitted. Something else must be going on. But what?

Circling wide, Zoe thought she glimpsed several dark figures fading into the trees at the edge of the parking lot. Freya zeroed in on the distant forms and did her best to drag her handler closer.

Out of the corner of her eye, Zoe saw a flash of white. Angel was on her way, too. One dog might be mistaken, but both were probably right. The struggling at the edge of the lot involved their missing little friend. He hadn't wandered away. He'd been kidnapped again!

Every nerve in her body fired, driving her forward at a run. She hadn't heard any shots. But if she didn't get to Patrick before his father did, Sean could fall into the same deadly trap he'd avoided the last time. Surely he must realize that, yet he was still running toward danger.

He was gaining, on her right, trying to keep pace with the barking, straining border collie.

Zoe pulled her gun and shouted, "Stay back."

Sean ignored her. All he seemed to care about was Patrick. Reaching him was his only goal.

At that point, Zoe broke a rule, praying she wasn't making a terrible mistake, and let go of Freya's leash. The Belgian Tervuren took off as if she were rocket propelled, paws barely touching the ground, fur flying, teeth bared.

Zoe was close enough to see a gun barrel rising. The muzzle-flash came fractions of a second later. Her heart had already been hammering. When she saw someone fire at her beloved K-9 partner, she thought it might pound right out of her chest.

Freya never faltered. She hit the shooter hard,

carrying him back and down, then standing on his chest and growling into his face, mere inches away. He tried to bring his pistol to bear on her again.

Gasping, Zoe pushed the last few feet. The gun was rising. Aiming at Freya. She wasn't going escape injury this time!

In a flurry of fur and shouting, a booted foot kicked the man's arm hard enough that she heard the cast crack. He screamed. Angel joined Freya by crunching down on the already broken arm and shaking it the way she would a rat.

That fit. The rat was human, and he was down and disarmed. That left only whoever was restraining Patrick.

Zoe trained her gun on the prostrate shooter and ordered, "Freeze," while Sean picked up the man's gun and pointed it at the other adult.

A crowd from the pageant had followed and was beginning to gather close by. Someone shone a beam of light on Patrick and his captor. It was a woman. She wasn't elderly, nor was she as young as Zoe. Her clothing was pristine. Her hair perfectly coiffed. Her nails manicured. She would have presented a comforting picture if not for the look in her eyes. It radiated pure evil.

"Alice! What are you doing here?" Sean shouted.

"I came for my grandson."

"You can't have him."

"Oh, really?" she snorted derisively. "It looks like I already do."

"You know what I mean." Sean lowered the gun rather than take the chance he'd accidentally harm Patrick.

"I know more than that," Alice screeched. "Now all your friends will know it, too. You don't care for this boy. You just want control of his fortune."

"What fortune?"

"Ha! You can't fool me. You know all about the trust. Sandra left everything to her son. She told you. I know she did. She said so before she died."

"I have no idea what you're talking about. Sandra was so confused after she got hooked on drugs she told wild stories all the time. I quit paying attention long ago."

"Liar!" Alice's grip on the boy tightened. She brandished a knife and pressed it against the side of his small neck.

Sean put down the assailant's gun and held up both hands, palms out, to demonstrate submission. "I'm not armed. You don't need that knife."

She gestured at the man on the ground. "Give him back his gun and back off."

When Sean's glance met Zoe's he knew that wasn't going to happen. It was a standoff. He looked around. "Get these kids out of here so they don't have to watch. You, too, Maisy. Patrick will be all right. Go back to the pageant."

The girl was sobbing to Alice. "Please let him go."

"He'll have a wonderful life with me and my husband. And he won't have to worry about his crazy daddy," the older woman shouted back.

Sean's fists clenched. If not for the knife at his son's throat, he'd jump her and end this. Since Patrick could easily be cut, he had to hold himself in check. He had to.

Flashes of invisible light nearly blinded him. Mortar shells exploded. Sean shut his eyes and covered his ears against the mental bombardment of war. All he could think, all he could do, was call out to the God he had denied and pray from the heart. So he did.

There was no instant relief, but he did begin to breathe more slowly, to feel a sense of encroaching peace. It was as if he were an outside observer, watching a life-and-death struggle over which he had no control.

Blinking, he forced his eyes to open. To focus. Alice was still holding Patrick, still grimacing as if she were readying herself to plunge the knife despite her need to keep her grandson alive.

"If—if you hurt him, you'll never get custody," Sean managed to choke out.

"I will if you're dead. That was the original plan, but those idiots I hired failed."

"Suppose I sign over the trust. Will that do?"

"You can't. That's not legal. We'd been administering it for Sandra, and we'll keep doing it for the boy."

Sean was desperate. He shouted, "I don't want any money! Got that? You can have it all. Just let go of my son."

"You can end this right here and now," Alice said. "If your cop buddies won't let my associate shoot you, you can shoot yourself."

During the time in the past when he had initially struggled to regain his mental equilibrium, Sean had toyed with the idea of suicide. Now, he had somehow crossed a line and desperately wanted to live. To make a new life and begin to enjoy it. That's what his counselors had tried to tell him during his darkest hours. There was life and happiness and a future waiting on the other side of his illness. To have purposely ended his life carly would have been a selfish, foolish act that would have hurt his loved ones beyond measure.

Nevertheless, he could pretend to agree to stall for time. Surely the officers who had been at the church tonight must be getting ready to act.

Zoe shouted, "No!" as he lifted the gun slightly.

While Alice was holding tight to Patrick, her attention was on Sean, so the deranged grandmother failed to see what was happening behind her. A few armed officers, in and out of uniform, had cut off her escape. That was a start. All Sean had to figure out was how to get her to release the boy without harming him.

The sight of his border collie, Angel, creeping along on her belly like a commando startled him. He knew that breed instinctively herded animals, but he'd never seen her crawl before. Not only was she sneaking up on Alice, she was getting away with it! Above all, he must not let himself give away the dog's position by staring at her.

A glance at Zoe told him she had seen Angel, too. Was it possible? Could the intelligent dog be acting on her own to end the stalemate? It sure looked that way.

"Well?" Alice screeched, obviously near her breaking point. "What are you waiting for?"

His arm raised a little more. The older woman began to smile. Angel was almost in position. Was she going to succeed in distracting Alice? The idea seemed preposterous to Sean until he remembered his tortuous, rambling, silent prayer.

A deep breath preceded a whispered, "Please, God," just as the dog's jaws clamped hard on Alice's ankle the way they would have on the hock of a misbehaving sheep.

She screamed, let go of the boy and slashed wildly at the attacking canine.

Angel was quicker. She ducked, parried and ran back to deliver a second nip before dashing off again and barking.

Officers reached Alice and restrained her. Sean

shoved the unfired gun at Zoe. Patrick dived for his father and ended up grasped tightly, lovingly.

As father and son embraced, Sean felt the arms of a third party wrapping around them. Zoe's tears of relief mingled freely with theirs, and the rightness of the moment was inescapable.

She was kissing his cheek. He turned his head slightly and did what he'd been yearning to do ever since their reunion. He finally kissed her properly. Seriously. And oh, so lovingly.

It was not only the best kiss he'd ever experienced, but her eager response proved that he hadn't made a mistake. The only difficulty was stepping away when the police were ready to clear the scene.

ELEVEN

Zoe kept remembering Sean's kiss and wondering if he had merely been reacting to the emotions of the rescue. The more she thought about it, the more confused she became.

By the time they were finished with their debriefing at the police station, Alice had been booked, as had her remaining hired thug. Her husband, John, had been notified and had disavowed any knowledge of her scheme to usurp the trust, one way or another. It was not up to the Desert Valley Police Department to ascertain whether or not he was telling the truth, since that part of the crime had occurred in another state.

Zoe covered a yawn on the way to the truck. "Sorry."

"You're entitled. It's been a long night."

The child sleeping against his shoulder stirred. "For all of us."

"Right. The hero dogs, too. I'm so glad they weren't hurt."

Smiling at the memories, she bent to pet them both. "No kidding. I was sure Freya had been shot. And when Angel bit your mother-in-law, I almost fell over. That's the way her breed handles sheep, but I never dreamed she was smart enough to put her instincts to use the way she did."

"Speaking of being smart," Sean said, "I have something I want to discuss with you. Everything that happened tonight made me realize how important it is. I'm just not sure how to put it."

"Simply would be best."

"Okay. I think you and I should get married."

"Whoa! After one kiss? I admit it was amazing, but that's a little too simple."

"What I mean is, Patrick needs a mother and you're fond of him, right?"

Zoe didn't like the way this was developing. "Yes."

"Well? I've talked to Dalton about applying for a job with his family's construction company, so I won't be freeloading. He says I can work outside and even pick my job sites, so you can go back to your position in Mesa without any conflicts if that's what you want."

"You've worked it all out, haven't you?"

There was hope in his expression. "I think so. How about it?"

Zoe almost choked up when she shook her head and said, "No."

"No? I'm getting better. You said so yourself. And I thought…"

"What? What did you think, Sean? That I'd sign up for a lifetime with you because I felt sorry for your son?"

"No, I…"

If she'd had any way to escape being with him, she'd have taken it. Unfortunately, they had ridden to the church and later to the station together.

Head lowered to hide her silent tears, Zoe turned away.

Sean opened the truck door, belted Patrick in safely, then straightened and placed both hands on her shoulders. "Something tells me I need to start over."

She didn't move. Could barely breathe.

He turned her to face him, continuing to hold her in place while he said, "I love you, Officer Trent. Probably always have, but I was too dense to realize it. I know we can make a marriage work. I just can't bear the thought of losing you again, especially since God went to so much trouble to bring us together."

"Go back," she said haltingly. "You love me?"

"With all my heart. I thought that kiss proved it."

"And you want to marry me?"

"More than anything."

Beginning to grin, Zoe slipped her arms around

his neck and tilted her face. "Why didn't you say so in the first place?"

Sean's initial answer was the second best kiss she'd ever had. When she finally leaned back to gaze into his eyes, she saw her old friend looking back at her. His spirit was still in there, still alive, and he loved her.

There was nothing more she could want. No other prayers that remained unanswered. He'd made his peace with God, and that would help him make peace with his traumatized mind. In the meantime, she'd be by his side, supporting his efforts. She and Angel.

"Then, yes," Zoe whispered. "I love you, too, Sean. I'll marry you." Her tender gaze swept past farther to his sleeping son and lingered as she began to smile. "Both of you."

"That's the best Christmas present I've ever received," Sean said.

Zoe smiled. "Me, too."

* * * * *

Dear Reader,

This story involves a father and son, both of whom have been hurt and are still battling to recover.

I realize that life does not always turn out the way we intended, but that doesn't mean it's not worthwhile. We each have a place in God's plans and are *all* valuable to Him. Approaching challenges and facing shortcomings is never easy, but I know from personal experience that it's better if we turn to God, to Jesus, for support. Just ask.

Special thanks to the other authors involved in this Rookie K-9 Unit series. They have all been a joy to work with. And to the long-suffering editors who brought us together and saw us through.

Blessings,

Valerie Hansen

HOLIDAY HIGH ALERT

Lenora Worth

To my dear friend and fellow writer Valerie Hansen.
Thank you for your guidance and your friendship!

And the work of righteousness shall be peace; and the effect of righteousness quietness and assurance forever.
–Isaiah 32:17

ONE

Desert Valley Day care was quiet now.

Then why did she keep hearing things?

Josie Callahan did one more check, but all of the children and the rest of the staff had gone home. All but one. Once rookie K-9 Officer Dalton West came to pick up his ten-year-old daughter, Maisy, all of the children, ranging from six months to twelve years old, would be home with their parents. Dalton had completed the winter K-9 training session but had decided to stay in town until after the holidays to gain more experience and fill in for some of the senior officers.

Tired, Josie shook off the creepy feeling and went about shutting down the building. She typically didn't allow any of the staff to stay here alone, including herself, but she'd sent them all ahead tonight. Christmas was only a week and a half away, and everyone needed extra time to shop. But Dalton was running late. Nothing unusual there. The man lived for his work.

A piercing pain stabbed at her heart. She had no one to go home to, anyway.

A noise in the back parking lot sounded like a motor humming near the covered drop-off area. A car door slammed, the sharp sound echoing around the building. Footsteps pounded against the asphalt.

That might be Dalton now.

Wondering why he parked in the back, Josie glanced up the hallway to where Maisy sat reading a book in the big reception room. "Your dad's on his way, Maisy. I think I heard his car."

Maisy nodded and tugged at her long dark brown ponytail, her expression stoic. "He works too much."

"I know, honey. But he's one of the good guys. He has an important job. He's been training so hard, and now he's gaining even more experience helping out the local police."

"And he has Luna," Maisy replied, rubbing at her nose. "She makes him smile."

"You make him smile, too," Josie said, her heart turning to mush each time she thought of the handsome, no-nonsense widower who'd enrolled his daughter in the after-school program about three months ago. Luna, a brindle black-mouth cur with some chocolate Lab thrown in, was his K-9 partner. Luna was an expert tracker. Dalton and Luna were still considered rookies since they'd been partnered at the Canyon County K-9 Training Center for intensive training, but Josie could tell that Dalton West already knew his stuff. He'd been a detective in another town before he decided to become a K-9 officer. And he'd be going back to Flagstaff soon.

Listening, Josie heard a tap on the kitchen window. Dalton must be in a hurry. Not that she blamed him. He'd want to pick up his daughter and head home for the evening.

Josie hadn't locked the front door yet, but she'd locked the back one after she'd gone out and secured the playground gate. She headed to the back to let him in, Josie's thoughts returning to the dedicated police officer.

Dalton West didn't smile much, but he loved his little girl. And when he did smile at Maisy, Josie couldn't help but get caught up in seeing that love.

He had a beautiful smile.

Get back into the here and now. She'd have a rare night at home. Since her aunt, Marilyn Carter, who was also her partner in this new venture, had four rambunctious children, Josie always stayed for the late-shift workers if they had kids here after regular hours.

No one tonight, however. Just one girl awaiting her a-little-late father.

When she heard someone moving around outside again, she called out, "Coming, Dalton. Just let me check a few things."

She peeked into the various rooms, turning off

lights and checking cabinets to make sure the supplies were put away properly. Halfway to the back door, she heard heavy footsteps hitting the tiled walkway leading to the playground.

"I'm coming, Dalton," she called again, her hand on the door.

The door shook with a jarring flurry.

Impatient man! "Just a minute."

Her hand on the doorknob, Josie inserted the key into the dead bolt. But the front door swung open, causing her pulse to rush into high-speed.

She whirled. "Dalton?"

Maisy ran and hugged her daddy. Josie backed away from the door with a funny feeling. Needles of fear moved down her backbone. She thought she'd heard footsteps running away. Who'd been out there?

"Sorry I'm late," he said. Taking Maisy by the hand, he strolled toward the kitchen, his alert gaze raking over Josie. "Hey, you okay?"

She forced a nod, glancing toward the playground. "Yes, I'm fine. I thought you were at the back door."

"No. I parked out front."

"Someone was there," she said. "They shook the door handle several times. I'm worried they were trying to break in."

"Do you have any other kids here?" Dalton asked, his gray eyes darkening as he went on alert.

"No, just Maisy," Josie replied. "Maybe someone thought their child was still here."

"But they know to call you on your cell," he said, well aware of the rules.

"I'm sure it was nothing," Josie said for Maisy's benefit, trying to hide the shudder moving down her spine. "Maybe someone got the wrong address."

Dalton gently shoved Maisy toward Josie. "You two stay here. Luna and I will take a look."

Josie didn't argue. They were all still jittery after one of the new kids at the day care, six-year-old Patrick Murphy, had almost been kidnapped by his maternal grandmother.

Josie was still shaken by that episode, which had happened the night of the Christmas pageant at the church, so she was probably overreacting. The grandmother hadn't come here to snatch Patrick, but Josie couldn't afford for the parents to think the day care might not be completely safe. Patrick stayed here almost every day, and his dad, Sean, trusted her to take care of Patrick since the boy had special needs.

"Is there a criminal out there?" Maisy asked, her gray-blue eyes full of fear.

"I don't think so," Josie replied, her tone steady in spite of her heart's constant bumping. Maisy knew as much police lingo as anyone, and the girl had a keen awareness that broke Josie's heart.

"Your daddy wants to be sure everything is okay before we go home."

Maisy held her book tightly to her midsection. "A criminal killed my mom."

Josie bent, her hands on Maisy's slender arms. "I know and I'm so sorry. But your daddy is trained to help us with things like that."

"Then why didn't he save my mom?" Maisy asked, her solemn expression full of despair.

Josie had a degree in education and a minor in child care administration, but she didn't know how to answer that question. So she went with her instincts. "Your daddy tried his best to help your mom, Maisy. But sometimes, no matter how hard we try, we can't save the people we love."

"He's making up for it," Maisy said. "He wants to keep us safe. I try to be good all the time so he won't worry."

Josie inhaled a breath. Maisy had probably never told her daddy these things. "Yes, he does want to keep you safe." Touching a finger to Maisy's nose, she added, "But you, Miss Maisy, don't need to try to be good. Your daddy knows you are one of a kind. He loves you so much."

And, yes, he was making up for not getting to his wife in time. She'd heard the horrible story about how a drug dealer had broken into their home looking for Dalton, who'd been an under-cover detective in Flagstaff at the time. Instead, they'd found his wife and taken her, leading to a high-speed chase that ended with the car flipping and his wife being killed. Thankfully, Maisy had hidden in a bathroom.

When she heard Dalton coming back inside, Luna with him and in her official K-9 vest, Josie hugged Maisy close. "We'll be okay, honey."

Maisy clung tightly to Josie. Then she looked up at Josie and whispered, "I'm the one who has to make sure he's okay."

Dalton gave Luna the space to do her job, the leash loose in his hand until they moved toward the back of the house. When they reached Josie and his daughter, Luna immediately let out a low yelp in greeting to her best buddy.

"Hey, Luna," Maisy said, reaching to pet the dog's brown-and-gold brindle coat.

"She has to work now," Dalton explained. Glancing at Josie, he nodded. "Unlock the door and then take Maisy to the front of the house. I'll need the playground keys, too."

She nodded, her green eyes full of trust in spite of the frown marring her heart-shaped face. "I'm sure it's nothing." Her gaze moved to Maisy in a warning, the curve of her auburn bangs shadowing her expression.

"No, a precaution," he said to reassure both of them. "Standard procedure, right, Maisy?"

Maisy stared up at her dad with solemn eyes. "If you say so."

"I say so." He waited for Josie to turn the lock. "This won't take long, and then we can order a pizza and call it a day."

"Can Miss Josie come with us?" Maisy asked in a tone full of hope underlined by demand.

Dalton's gaze clashed with Josie's. "Uh...we'll have to see. Let me take care of this, and then we'll talk."

His daughter, the little matchmaker.

Dalton leaned down to Luna. "Search, girl," he ordered.

Luna took off, her head lifting up, her nostrils flaring. Then she lowered her head to the ground around the door before running toward the chain-link fence that enclosed the playground area across from the drop-off driveway.

Luna turned away from the fence, her nose going back down on the ground now. She followed the driveway all the way to the street and then whined an alert.

"They were in a vehicle," Dalton noted, his gaze scanning the street that ran along the left back side of the Tudor-style building.

They must have driven up to the drop-off area and gotten out to check the back door. Anyone could have pulled up to the door and touched the handle. Maybe a child had lost something and a parent had come looking, thinking the whole place was locked up. Thankfully, the door had been locked.

"I need something solid," he said to Luna.

They went back over the entire yard, even the playground area they'd skirted before. Dalton unlocked the gate to the playground, careful to hold Luna's leash around one wrist. It didn't look as if the lock had been tampered with. He could dust for prints, but there had to be hundreds on the door handle. He'd need something more isolated and specific.

He followed Luna around the playground, past the swings and climbing gyms. The muscular dog halted at the corner of the fence where an outcrop jutted high enough for someone to make it over the heavy, wooden security fence.

"Parked on the street, came to the door and then managed to sneak around the corner to hop this fence to get into the playground?" Luna moved through the rubber mulch under the various gym sets, castles and curving slides. She stopped short near one of the smaller forts, her nose sniffing at something lying on the mulch inside the miniature enclosure.

A white folded piece of paper, taped together.

Dalton dug in his equipment belt for a pair of plastic gloves. Telling Luna to stay, he let go of the leash and pulled the gloves over his hands before picking up the heavy-grade paper.

It was addressed to Josie Callahan.

Josie sat with Maisy, talking about anything to keep the little girl's mind off what was going on out in the backyard.

"Yes, this used to be someone's home," she explained. "But this whole area was rezoned for commercial use."

"What does that mean?" Maisy asked, her backpack right by her feet. The child was very precise about her belongings.

"It means that the town allowed this building to be used for a business instead of a home. I moved to Desert Valley to be close to my aunt, and when we found this huge old house for sale, we changed it into an official day care for children."

"Mrs. Carter," Maisy supplied. "Your aunt is nice."

"Yes, she is. And she loves children." Josie was thankful for her aunt Marilyn and thankful that Desert Valley was a long way from the small Texas town where she'd lived all of her life. A town she'd been forced to leave. "She watched children in her home, and since I'd always wanted to do that, too, we decided to open our own place. This building always reminded me of a gingerbread house, so we thought it would be perfect for children."

Maisy gave her a rare smile. "I love coming here."

"Me, too," Josie admitted with pride. "We worked hard to make it perfect."

They'd hired a contractor, gutted walls, installed the necessary equipment to bring it up to code and had gone through lots of forms and permits to make their day care a reality.

"I hope my dad's okay," Maisy said, craning her neck to see down the hallway.

Before Josie could come up with a reassuring answer, she heard the back door swing open and then the *tap, tap* of Luna's nails hitting the tile.

"There they are now," she said, releasing the breath she'd been holding.

"Daddy, is it okay to go out?" Maisy asked, jumping up.

Josie could hear the tremor of fear in the girl's question.

"It's safe," Dalton said. "But I do need to talk to Miss Josie."

"Can I hear?"

"Why don't you read your book for a bit more," Dalton said in a firm tone. "Then we'll figure out dinner."

Josie didn't like that tone. It meant he needed to speak to her in private.

"A word in the office," he suggested. Then he turned to Luna. "Stay with Maisy."

Luna dropped to the floor and stared up at Maisy with adoring brown eyes.

Dalton escorted Josie across to the office through what used to be the living-dining area. They could see Maisy and Luna through the glass window.

"I found this on the playground near one of the slides," he said.

When she saw her name spelled out in cutout letters on the folded sheet, she inhaled a deep breath. "Someone left this for me?"

"It looks that way," he said. He handed her a pair of latex gloves. "Put these on and open it."

Josie did as he asked, her heart pounding so hard the lace on her blouse kept fluttering. When she saw the cutout words pasted against the stark white, her heart took off again.

Who so sheddeth man's blood, by man shall his blood be shed. Genesis 9:6 (The wicked shall pay.)

Dalton's gray-eyed gaze met hers. Josie saw the concern in his expression.

Then he leaned in and lowered his voice. "This is obviously about more than a parent dropping by after hours. This was deliberate. And if I hadn't arrived when I did, you and Maisy could have been in serious danger."

TWO

"Daddy, I'm ready for pizza."

Josie carefully folded the paper and pivoted when she saw Maisy standing at the office door. "Your dad will be done soon, honey."

Maisy's big eyes widened. "Are you coming with us, Miss Josie? Please?"

Josie didn't know how to answer that. She didn't want to disappoint Maisy but…she had no business going to eat pizza with these two. She knew to keep her professional life and her personal life separated. "I…uh…"

"I have an idea," Dalton said, his eyes bright for Maisy's sake. "How about we follow Miss Josie home and we can order pizza from her house."

Josie sent him a shocked, questioning glare, her thoughts rolling over each other. "Really?"

"Really," he said. "It never hurts to see where my daughter's favorite after-school teacher lives. You know, to make sure things are okay?"

He wanted to check her home?

The dread Josie felt over the last few minutes increased twofold. Her stomach knotted, and her breath stopped cold. She rambled on, trying to recover. "It's been a while since I've had any company besides my aunt and uncle. I moved in next to them after Whitney married David and moved to a bigger house."

Whitney was also a K-9 officer and her husband, David, was a physician's assistant planning to go back to med school to become a full-fledged doctor. They lived around the corner in a new subdivision and were raising Whitney's little daughter, Shelby, a regular here at the day care.

"I'd heard that," he responded, his tone neutral and calm. "I'd like to see where you live."

He wasn't leaving her room to say no. Maybe it was a good idea to have him do a sweep, in case. In case of what? She didn't want to think about that.

"Of course," she said. "Let me finish locking up."

"And Luna's coming, too," Maisy said, her tone truly happy for a change. The young girl probably needed some motherly companionship.

"I wouldn't have it any other way," Josie said, thinking this was an interesting turn of events. And a disturbing one. She worried about what had happened, and for some reason she didn't want to examine too closely, she also fretted about being near Dalton West. The man cut an intimidating swath.

Just get home and think this through, she told herself. There had to be an explanation for that cryptic message.

And there had to be an explanation for the pitter-patter of her heart every time Dalton came to pick up Maisy.

Together she and Dalton double-checked the doors and windows. "All clear," he said after she'd locked the main entry. "I need to bag this letter, and then we'll be right behind you. I'll dust it for prints later. Might find some on the tape if not the paper."

After he'd settled Luna in her backseat kennel and Maisy in the front, seat belt secured, he turned to Josie. "I'm going to watch the streets between here and your house. And when the pizza comes, I'll answer the door. Better to be cautious than careless," he added. "I'm following you home and that's that. And we can talk about what might have provoked this."

"I'll see you there, then."

"Be careful," he said. She felt him watching her until she was in her car.

What a bossy man! No, more than bossy. Serious and commanding. Trustworthy. Good at his job. Josie sent up a prayer of thanks. Dalton had probably saved her from a break-in or a possible robbery. She should be relieved. Someone had pinpointed the day care and left that note for her to find.

Knowing that a police officer with a highly trained K-9 partner was following her home and coming inside to check her house made her feel a lot better about things. Because if she thought too long and hard about that note, she'd fall to pieces and… Josie wasn't going to give in to that notion.

She wasn't that woman anymore.

Dalton eased the old patrol car against the curb in front of the little house where Josie lived next to her aunt and uncle. The Carters were good people. Marilyn loved children, and her husband, Jack, ran his own auto repair company and worked on keeping all the old patrol cars running smoothly.

Josie Callahan obviously had the same work ethic as her relatives. He'd heard the stories about the old rambling house that was now the day care. Whitney and David had recommended it to Dalton when he'd needed after-school care for Maisy. And not a moment too soon. They moved here not long after the day care had opened.

A good idea since everyone around here needed a safe place to leave their children. He especially considered the place an answer to his prayers since he didn't like leaving Maisy alone in the house, even with a nanny or teenage sitter. Maisy still had nightmares about her mother's death, so she needed to be in a safe and fun environment.

Up until now, he'd believed the Desert Valley Day care had been that place. But after Patrick Murphy's close call a couple of weeks ago with a vindictive, unhinged grandmother who thought he should be with her instead of his dad, Sean, and now this situation, he needed to find out what was going on.

Why would someone target the day care? Or rather, why would someone target Josie Callahan?

"This is a cute house," Maisy said, all smiles since they'd pulled into the neighborhood. "Look at the lights, Daddy."

"I see," Dalton responded. The lone fake Christmas tree he and Maisy had decorated a few weeks ago looked sad compared to this display.

The little beige stucco cottage was neat and clean. A small rock garden in front held a scrawny palm tree with top-heavy fronds and several varieties of cactus bushes, all of which were decorated with colorful Christmas lights. A pretty tree stood at the front window, and a palm-tree-embellished wreath hung on the front door. The woman must have a thing for desert palms.

But Dalton wasn't focused on the decorations. He glanced around the neighborhood, checking the cul-de-sac and scanning the street. A few vehicles were parked here and there, but he couldn't see anything that looked suspicious. Leashing Luna, he ordered her out, and they all headed up the drive to meet Josie at the door.

"Come in," she said, her tone unsure. "I have some pizza coupons."

Dalton scooted Maisy ahead of him, noting she had her favorite purple backpack. That thing seemed to be her security blanket these days. Luna followed, sniffing the new location with interest, her dark eyes full of curiosity.

Dalton scanned the tiny den and kitchen, making sure nothing was out of order. Neat and sparse with old but tidy wicker furniture and one big, comfortable-looking, puffy beige side chair. He watched as Josie moved around and fluffed pillows, her actions guarded.

"Make yourself comfortable," she said, clearly *uncomfortable*.

Maybe he shouldn't have forced the issue, but he couldn't shake the wariness gnawing at the pit of his stomach.

Regardless, they were here now so he'd do his job.

"Thanks." He motioned to Maisy. "Sit down, honey. You can put your pack on the coffee table."

Maisy did as he told her, her big gray-blue eyes gazing around the room with delighted interest. At least his daughter was enjoying this diversion.

Now Dalton had to wonder what had really prompted him to insist on coming to dinner at Josie's house. That threatening note, of course. Someone had gone to a lot of trouble to plant that. What if a kid had found it? Depending on what the kid would do with the note, Josie might have never known about it or the whole day care could have gone into a panic.

Both dangerous concepts.

He needed to follow through and get that note to the lab, but Dalton doubted anything substantial would be found on the paper. He might be able to question Josie after dinner if they could find a distraction for Maisy and Luna.

"Your place looks nice," he said when Josie came over with her cell phone and a handful of coupons. "Whitney loved it here, but she and David are happy in their new house from what I hear."

"That's good," Josie said. "Whitney told me they went through the wringer when they first met." Glancing at Maisy, she smiled. "But they made it through."

Dalton nodded, glad she didn't go into detail in front of his daughter about drug dealers and the town doctor who'd turned bad. "Yeah, they seem very happy."

"Shelby is so cute," Maisy said, clearly interested in the adult conversation. "She's funny when she walks. She falls and then gets right back up."

"She loves to run, but sometimes her feet get ahead of her," Josie said. "Even at eighteen months, she's a go-getter like her mama."

The silence that followed seemed like an eternity. Dalton wished he'd thought this through a little better. He'd never been one for small talk. "Pizza time," he finally said. "Want me to order?"

"No, I'll do it." Josie went through the various coupons, and they settled on toppings and a nearby restaurant that delivered. "One large pepperoni and sausage and one medium veggie," she told the restaurant clerk.

After she'd given the address and placed her phone down, she turned to Maisy. "I have water and milk to drink."

"Milk," Maisy said, shy now.

"Do you have homework?" Dalton asked Maisy.

She bobbed her head. "Reading. Miss Josie helped me with the math."

"But you might want to let your dad go over that with you since I'm a bit rusty," Josie suggested. "She's very smart in math," she said to Dalton. "She even explained a few things to me."

Proud to hear that, Dalton smiled at Maisy. "Okay, after we eat you can read for a while, and I'll check the math when we get home." But he doubted that would be necessary. Josie seemed like a capable woman. Pretty and smart. But what else was going on there?

Satisfied with his suggestion, Maisy became curious. "I like your house, Miss Josie. Our house is boring."

Dalton gave her a mock-affronted frown. "Did you say boring? I beg your pardon. Our house is warm and safe and...boring."

Maisy giggled and got up to walk around. "We don't have all the pretty decorations." She pointed to a picture of a grinning snowman. "Does it ever snow here?"

"Yes," Josie said, smiling at Maisy. "It gets really cold here at times, too, like Flagstaff where you usually live. Do you like snow?"

Maisy glanced at Dalton. "Yes, sometimes. The day my mom died, it was snowing. But...we didn't get to go out and play in it."

Josie gave Dalton a sympathetic look, her green eyes full of understanding. "Maybe we'll get snow for Christmas," she said. "I'll take you outside, and we'll make snowballs."

"And a snowman," Maisy replied, content once more.

Dalton's heart shattered all over again at the pain he heard in his daughter's words. Would Maisy ever be able to forget that day over a year ago when her mom had been taken from them? He didn't want to remember that day, and he only wished Maisy could wipe it out of her mind, too.

"I'm going to take Luna for a walk," he said. Anything to get away from the pity in Josie's eyes and the hurt in his little girl's heart. Then he shot Josie a signal and mouthed, "We'll check things outside."

She nodded and got Maisy involved in helping her find plates and napkins. Their chatter echoed after him when Dalton shut the front door, Luna by his side.

Taking in the cold night air, he breathed deeply and closed his eyes. The dark memories threatened to overtake him, but Dalton had learned through counseling to work through the memories and to focus on seeing his daughter whole and happy again. Being with Josie did make Maisy laugh, at least.

And Lord, make me whole and happy again, too, he prayed.

Maybe the one prayer he asked for Maisy's sake every day had led him to come to Josie's home tonight. Truth be told, he had a slight crush on the pretty brunette with the shimmering green eyes. She had a knockout smile and a warm heart. She was a good person and, well, she was easy on the eye. He hadn't noticed another woman since Eileen had died, but lately he'd noticed little things about Josie. Those little things added up to a whole package that he couldn't ignore.

Was he ready for that kind of thing? Probably not. Besides, he'd be heading back to Flagstaff after Christmas. He and Maisy could start fresh in a new house, and he'd have a new position as an official K-9 officer.

Dalton cleared his head. He had work to do and a little girl to take care of. No time for such nonsense.

But he couldn't get Josie's sweet smile and

the kind way she handled his daughter out of his mind. Someone had sent her what could be perceived as a threatening note. So he told Luna to search, and the slender dog took off like a rocket.

Doing her job without hesitation.

He needed to do the same.

They cleared the front and back yards and were headed back inside when Luna's head went up and a soft growl emitted from her throat. She sniffed the air, and her body turned toward the left. Dalton listened and glanced to the far end of the street, but a shrub blocked his view. Urging Luna forward, he saw a car he didn't remember from before. Too dark to see the make and model.

Dalton heard footsteps pounding, and then someone jumped into the car and took off in the other direction. Had that someone been watching Josie's house?

THREE

Josie glanced up when Dalton and Luna came back inside. "We're all ready. Any sign of the pizza guy?"

"No. Didn't run into anyone," he said, his alert gaze moving over the entire room before settling back on her. He looked distracted. "We'll keep watch," he added, his hand on the blinds covering the front window. "Maybe he'll be here soon, and then we can eat and get out of your hair."

Josie knew something was up, but she didn't say anything. "Okay, well, we can sit and talk or watch television until the pizza gets here."

"Talking is a good idea," Dalton said, turning to face her. "I'd like to get to know you better."

Josie sent him a questioning glance. The man had hardly spoken a complete sentence to her, other than to get Maisy registered and a quick "hello" and "thank you" here and there. "Sure. What would you like to know?"

"Where are you from?"

She didn't want to go down this road, but he was obviously trying to conduct an interrogation. "Texas, but you know that, right?"

"Where in Texas?"

"A town near Waco. Pine Cone."

"You lived in a town called Pine Cone?" Maisy asked with a giggle, her big eyes full of the same inquisitive perusal as her dad's.

Josie swallowed her fears. "Yes. It's so small it only has one traffic light and one main street. Pine Street."

Maisy shook her head and got out her reading book. "Must be a lot of pine trees around there."

"Yes. Tall, giant pines. Not quite as dainty as the ponderosa pines around here."

Josie motioned to Dalton. He ordered Luna to stay, and the big dog curled up next to Maisy. Then he walked over to the counter.

"What's with all the personal questions?" Josie asked.

"I'll need to gather some background information," Dalton said in a low voice.

"Why?"

He put both hands on the counter and stared at her with solemn gray eyes. "Relax. Just as a precaution."

"No," she said, anger and dread clawing at her throat. "You're going to do a background *check*, aren't you? I had to go through that process in order to open the day care and...everything checked out."

He tapped the counter. "If you're being threatened, I need to know who could be after you. Someone from home, maybe."

Josie didn't want to delve into thinking about anyone from home coming after her. She hadn't told anyone where she was going, and the people she'd known had to have forgotten her by now. Even her bitter, heartbroken and widowed mother-in-law Janine Callahan, who was too sick with grief to plot something like this.

"And why do you think it would be someone from Texas?" she countered, hoping he was wrong. She'd tried to keep her past in the past. "It could be an angry parent."

"Yes, that's true. Have you had a disagreement with any of the parents recently?"

Josie shook her head. "No. We've only been open a few months, and usually if a parent has a complaint, we handle it immediately and try to make it right. If we're aware of it."

He processed that for a minute and then said, "Maybe someone is upset with you or someone else at the day care, but they haven't shared that with you."

"Why would they go about things in this way?" she asked. "This seems extreme, considering we've had nothing but good reviews and our clients send people to us. You know that firsthand."

"I agree," he said. "I'm gathering facts, Josie. Not accusing you or anyone on your staff."

"Are you worried about a repeat of what happened with Patrick?" she asked, concerned about the little boy's abduction attempt. Maisy had been upset when Patrick went missing. The girl didn't need to worry about the happenings at the day care, too.

"That incident did come to mind," he replied. "But we know who tried to take Patrick."

"Okay," she said, inhaling to calm her nerves. But her home and business both now held a sinister sheen that reminded her of why she'd left Texas. "What do you think?"

"I don't know. It could be a prank, or it could be that they're after one of your employees. Anyone working with you having relationship problems? Any hint of domestic violence?"

"No," she said, wishing he'd back off. "You know my aunt. She's one of the nicest people in the world. Same with my uncle. We have four other workers who've all had extensive background checks, and they're all trained to work with children. They're good people. We were thorough in making sure they were suitable to work at the day care."

"I can believe that," he said. "Let's table this for now."

Thankfully, the doorbell rang. But Josie's heart

sped out of control and she jumped. Then she rushed around Dalton, a wad of cash in her hand.

"No, let me," he said, pulling out his wallet. "I want to check the delivery person, anyway."

"You don't trust my pizza delivery boy, either?"

"Right now, I don't trust anyone, and I'm here to make sure you don't let anyone you don't know into your house."

She'd let *him* in, Josie thought, ragged nerves making her want to scream. But that tension made her appreciate his strong presence. When he opened the door, her regular delivery person looked shocked to see the tall, dark-haired man standing there.

"Oh, hi…uh… Officer," the young man with bright red hair said. "How ya doing?" He glanced around Dalton and smiled at Josie. "Hey, Miss Callahan."

"Hey, Ryan. Good to see you."

Dalton paid the kid and added an extra five. "Thanks, buddy." Then he glanced up and down the street before he shut the door.

After he'd set the two pizza boxes on the counter, Josie leaned close. "You saw someone out there earlier, didn't you?"

He made sure Maisy wasn't listening and then nodded. "But it could have been a neighbor leaving in a hurry."

"Right," Josie said, wishing she could believe

that. "Let's eat before the pizza gets cold," she added to show a sign of bravado.

But she didn't feel brave. And she'd lost her appetite.

"Maybe you should stay next door tonight with your aunt," he suggested.

"I'm a grown woman. I won't let some random letter scare me."

He didn't like that response. "You need to take this seriously."

"Oh, I'm taking it seriously," she replied. "But...there's something you don't know about me, Dalton. I used to cower in fear and try to please everyone. But I've changed. I stand up for myself these days."

He passed out pizza and then stood there staring at her. "I'm glad you're stronger now, but... sometimes it's hard to stand up to someone who's dangerous and deranged. That can get you hurt or worse...killed."

Josie stared down at her pizza, embarrassment heating her skin. She was being insensitive. Dalton's wife had been killed. He was just trying to warn Josie to be careful.

Looking into his stormy eyes, she said, "Thanks for the warning. I'll...call my aunt and tell her what happened and... I'll be careful. I promise."

"Good." He smiled and called Maisy over to the dining table. "Let's eat, honey, and then we have to get home. You've got school tomorrow."

Josie touched his arm. "Thank you, Dalton, for doing this."

"My job," he said. "And… I have to take care of you. You're one of Maisy's favorite people."

Josie felt a new kind of shiver moving down her spine.

The kind a woman got when she realized she might be attracted to a good-looking man.

But she couldn't explore those feelings until she found out who had targeted her at her place of business today. That was urgent. But add to that, Dalton was moving back to Flagstaff in a couple of weeks. Nothing could happen between them.

The next morning, Dalton told Chief Ryder Hayes about what he'd found and showed him the letter, which he'd placed in a letter-sized mailing envelope.

"I dusted it for prints," he said, "but I didn't find anything traceable. So that means whoever left this must have been wearing gloves." He leaned back in his chair. "Josie will alert me if she receives anything else suspicious."

"Best you can do," Chief Hayes replied, his blue eyes pinning Dalton to the spot. "It could be random, but with kids involved, we can't take any chances. I don't want Lily in any danger."

Lily was the chief's little daughter. He'd lost his wife to a murderer a few years ago. They had that in common. But Ryder had found a second chance at love with Sophie, the lead K-9 trainer.

"I'm going to do background checks on everyone who works there," Dalton said. "And I plan to question all of them, too."

"Once a detective..." Chief Hayes smiled and nodded. "I hear Josie's a widow?"

"Yes, sir. She didn't mention that, but I'd heard it also."

Dalton wondered what had happened to her husband. She was awfully young to be a widow. Maybe he'd ask her about that.

Or maybe it was none of his business. He sure didn't like people asking what had happened to his wife.

He was happy for the chief, though. Ryder and Sophie planned to get married in February. Sophie had helped Dalton get acclimated to moving into a new area of law enforcement, and she'd shown him how to bond with Luna. Everyone here worked that way. As a team. He liked that.

Now he sat up and glanced at the chief. "Josie Callahan is a capable, hardworking woman. I can't imagine anyone wanting to come after her."

The chief's gaze hardened. "Part of our job is to be diligent and go with our gut. If you have a hunch that something isn't right, don't hesitant to follow through. Luna will know what to do."

"Yes, sir," Dalton replied.

After grabbing a corner desk, Dalton looked

up the Desert Valley Day care website and jotted down the names of the entire staff.

An hour later, he'd cleared several of the employees. Josie had been right. They were all highly qualified to work with children. No arrest reports or criminal activity. Most of them were female, ranging in age from twenty-five to fifty and educated in everything from child development to how to run a mother's-day-out program. One of them had even worked at the church in that capacity.

He'd saved Josie for last, maybe because he felt guilty about checking up on her. But…everyone had a past, and, while he'd been thorough, he knew people from the past could come looking. That's how his wife had died. A drug dealer had come looking for Dalton and had taken Eileen instead. But someone had called 911 and the police had immediately spotted the car. Then a high-speed chase had ensued and…the doped-up driver had lost control of the vehicle. The car had crashed into a stand of ponderosa pines and exploded. The driver and Eileen had been killed.

Maisy had been left alone in the house after Eileen had urged her to run next door. Instead of leaving her mother, his brave daughter had hidden and called for help.

He'd heard the alert on the radio, but Dalton had arrived at the scene too late to save Eileen.

Dalton couldn't let that happen again. He might

have missed something that hadn't shown up on the internet search.

He was about to run the check on Josie when fellow rookie Zoe Trent walked in with her partner, Freya, a beautiful brown Belgian Tervuren with some black tips covering her fur. Zoe's long, shiny brown hair matched her partner's. It was a joke around here, but Zoe took it in stride.

"Hey," he said, smiling. "How's it going?"

"Good," she said. "How about you?"

"I can't complain. How's Sean liking his new job?" Sean Murphy was little Patrick's dad. The two had been through a lot.

Dalton's father ran West Construction out of Flagstaff, and Dalton had suggested Zoe's new fiancé, Sean Murphy, get in touch with him to find work. West Construction had offices all over Arizona. Sean was now a regular on the construction crew that worked all over Canyon County. New construction was booming right now, so Sean stayed busy. Since Zoe had been assigned to go back to Mesa once the holidays were over, Sean could easily find work there, too.

Zoe sank down on a chair, Freya at her feet. Luna gave her K-9 friend a lift of the head and a little woof. Freya stared at the other dog and gave a doggie smile in acknowledgment.

"He loves building houses," Zoe said. "Thank you so much for recommending him to your dad. This job is good therapy for his PTSD since your dad doesn't mind his service dog, Angel, being on-site."

"I'm glad it worked out," Dalton replied. Sean Murphy had been injured by an IED while serving in Afghanistan.

Proud of how his family supported returning veterans, he said, "I haven't talked to my folks in a couple of weeks. I'll see them after the holidays since I'm pinch-hitting for some of the other officers."

It didn't feel like Christmas, but he had to keep his spirits up for Maisy's sake. "Sounds like you and Sean are happy."

Zoe's smile said it all. "Great. Better than great. And Patrick is amazing."

Dalton missed that kind of contentment in his own life. When he thought of Josie Callahan, his mind went back to work mode. Changing the subject, he said, "What's up today?"

"We've been going through our paces out on the practice yard at the training center," Zoe said, motioning to Freya. "What're you working on?"

Dalton gave her the specifics. "Strange and certainly a matter of concern."

"Sean won't like hearing this about the day care after what we went through with Patrick, but it might turn out to be nothing much."

"I hope so," Dalton replied. "I'm keeping close to this one, though. Maisy was there alone with Josie Callahan last night."

"I understand," Zoe said. "Let me know if you need me to pick up Maisy or do any groundwork on the case."

After he and Zoe caught up a little more, his cell rang.

"Dalton, it's Josie Callahan."

She sounded out of breath and upset.

"Are you okay?"

"No," she said. "We found another note."

"I'm on my way," Dalton replied, his gut burning.

Luna sensed his agitation and fell in right beside him. Together they hurried out to his patrol car.

FOUR

Josie held the manila envelope away, staring at it as if it might be a bomb. Her fingerprints were all over it. But she'd found some gloves in the nursery and now she could feel her palms sweating against the sticky latex.

But the words made her go cold.

And my wrath shall wax hot, and I will kill you with my sword. Exodus 22:24

The verse had been taken out of context, but Josie got the meaning loud and clear. One note was questionable. Two made it real.

"Miss Josie, are you okay?" her assistant, Heather, asked from the office door, her hazel eyes bright with questions.

Josie dropped the envelope and the offending note made with cutout letters. "I'm going through the mail. Did you happen to notice when the mailman came?"

Heather shook her head, her brown ponytail bouncing. "No, ma'am. We've had people in and out all day. Did you find the envelope with your name on it?"

"Yes," Josie said, trying to stay calm. "I saw it with the mail. Did someone drop it off?"

"I found it wedged inside the door when I opened this morning," Heather replied. "I thought one of the parents left it."

Josie took a breath. "Thank you. Did you need something?"

Heather stood inside the doorway. "I wanted to check on you. You look tired."

Josie forced a smile. "I am tired. I didn't sleep very much last night but…it's nothing."

"Well, I'm about to take my lunch break, unless you need to go first."

"No, you go ahead," Josie said. She saw the police cruiser pulling up. "There's one of our parents now. I have a conference with Dalton West."

Heather grinned and glanced out the window. "He's a tall drink of water, as my mama likes to say."

Josie managed a tight smile. "Yes, he sure is. You go on and enjoy your lunch. I'll take the late shift."

Heather nodded and greeted Dalton as he appeared in the doorway to Josie's office, then glanced down at Luna. "Hey, there, Luna. Are you fighting crime today?"

Luna glanced at Dalton and then back at Heather, her nose in the air.

"We're on the job," Dalton said, his cheerful tone belying the panic Josie couldn't stop.

Dalton hurried into the office and shut the door. "Show me the note."

She handed him the manila envelope with her name scrolled on it in scraggly bold black. Then she pointed to the folded piece of paper lying beside it.

Dalton pulled a pair of gloves from his equipment belt and opened the envelope. After reading the words pasted there, he looked at her with a stoic stare. "This is serious."

"I'm not sure how to handle it."

"You have to be careful," Dalton replied, his gaze on the note. "Was this sealed?"

"No. Pressed together with the metal fastener. I opened it without gloves. It was with the mail, and I didn't even bother looking at the front."

"The mailman wouldn't have let this get through without a complete address," Dalton said.

"Heather found it by the front door early this morning and put it with the mail. What should I do? I can't allow the children to be in danger, and if I tell the parents, they'll take their children out of my care."

"We'll take it a step at a time. Right now, you're the target, but if it escalates we'll have to warn everyone. How did your aunt take it?"

"She had a doctor's appointment today, so

I haven't told her." She sank back in her chair and rubbed her forehead. "I'm concerned about the children."

Dalton placed the note back into the envelope. "Stay calm for now. I'll check the yard again, and I'll dust this the same as I did the last one. But I'm pretty sure we won't find anything. Do you have surveillance cameras?"

"We can't afford those. We have locks on the windows and doors and the playground gates. But they got inside the playground." She glanced out the window, thoughts of someone creeping around causing her to shiver. "My maintenance man is trying to remove that rock embedded by the fence."

"Well, there's no sign of break-ins. We can put a cruiser on the street to watch for anyone suspicious. Have them circle the block every few minutes after hours."

Josie had the certain sinking sensation that this person would find a way around a patrol car. "Okay. Then what?"

"I think we might want to go ahead and talk to the staff, Josie," he finally said. "I'd planned on questioning them about the first note, but I didn't want to alarm them. If we get them all together, maybe I can scope the room, get a feel for things. Luna can help there, too."

"You think someone on my staff could be doing this?"

"Can't rule anyone out," he replied. "Can you get them all together for a few minutes after closing?"

"I'll try," she said. "Besides my aunt, one other person has the day off."

That got his attention. "Who?"

"Tricia Munson. She works with the babies."

"Why did she take the day off?"

"To attend a funeral," Josie said, ruling out Tricia immediately. But Dalton didn't look so sure. The man must have been a great detective because he had a bulldog's tenacity.

"Who died?"

"Her uncle."

"Did he live here?"

"Yes," Josie said. "His obituary was in the paper this morning. Jeffery Munson. He's a highly respected local businessman."

Dalton must have sensed her disbelief. "I don't mean to sound insensitive," he said. "We have to start somewhere, and any employee acting out of the ordinary is fair game."

"I understand."

"Okay." He stood and held Luna's leash. "Get that meeting together for tonight."

"I'll tell Aunt Marilyn as soon as she gets back from her appointment."

"And I'll get that cruiser over here," Dalton said, his eyes a stormy gray. "Whoever this is, he's a coward. He comes after hours and in the dark of early morning. If I have to, I'll spend the night here. Luna will be glad to do that job."

The sleek dog glanced up at the sound of her name. She did look ready and willing. They both made Josie feel safe.

"Thank you," she said after she'd walked Dalton around the building. Luna didn't alert, so that was a relief. But she could tell the staff was beginning to wonder what was going on.

When they stopped in the front parking lot, Dalton did a scan of the entire yard. "You have a good open area, so nowhere for someone to hide. I'll be here on time to pick up Maisy this afternoon, and I'll do another sweep then."

"Okay," she said. She didn't want to depend on Dalton, but the man made her feel protected.

"I enjoyed last night," he said. "In spite of what brought us together."

"Pizza brought us together," she retorted, not wanting him to read anything into their dinner. "And your daughter's demands," she added with a smile.

He looked sheepish. "Yeah, sorry about that." Then he turned serious. "You spend a lot of time with Maisy. How is she doing, really?"

Josie chose her words carefully. "She misses her mom. Do you two ever talk about what happened?"

His expression hardened. "No. It's too hard to explain. We both went to counseling...after her mother died. I thought Maisy was doing better, but I know she has nightmares. So do I, for that matter."

Josie's heart went out to him. "It's tough. I still have nightmares about my husband's death."

Dalton latched on to that. "How did he die?"

She hadn't meant to say anything, but she trusted Dalton. "He worked at an oil refinery back in Texas. An accident that caused a chemical spill."

An accident that his family blamed on Josie because they considered her a bad wife. But they didn't know where she was now. She almost said something to Dalton, but the possibility of Douglas's mother or brother finding her was slim. His mother was sickly, and his brother had married and moved to Louisiana.

"That's tough," Dalton said. "Any coworkers who might have a grudge against him or you?"

She thought about that. "I didn't know the people he worked with, but...he'd come home with stories. Mostly gossip or news about their wives and children."

"Could you remember any of them?"

"We didn't socialize with them a lot." She grabbed a notepad from her purse. "Douglas mentioned George—George Cleveland—a lot. And Perry Wilcox. Perry was always mad about something and hated his job. Douglas used to go fishing with Rafael Gonzalez. He was a good man from what I remember." She handed him the list. "Douglas got into heated arguments with Perry. He told me Perry Wilcox was a hothead."

"We have to consider anyone who might have a grudge."

She'd blocked out that part of her life, and she didn't want to delve into it again. But she was willing to cooperate. "I hope it's not one of them."

He took another look around. "I have to go. But I'll be back for Maisy, and I'll send that patrol. Meantime, we have an incident file going, so document everything. The letters or anything else you might receive, the time of day, how and where. Keep your phone with you and… Josie, don't go anywhere alone. Call me if you need anything."

"Thanks again," Josie said, trying to absorb his instructions. She watched as he got in the squad car and sped away. Before, she'd always loved the front drive to the day care where she and her aunt had planted shrubs and palm trees and made pretty rock gardens filled with succulents. They'd worked hard to make the arched entryway to the heavy wooden front door welcoming and like a fun castle.

Now, she shivered in the cool breeze and searched the nearby businesses. The rambling day care building looked ominous and dark in spite of the wreath on the door.

When she came back inside, Heather was

standing in the hallway. "What was that all about, Miss Josie?"

"We're going to have a meeting tonight after work, and I'll explain," Josie said, paranoia new to her. "Meantime, it's work as usual."

"I don't mind a meeting," Heather retorted. "I was asking what's going on with you and that handsome lawman. He sure likes to look at you."

Josie scoffed at the notion, and then she shook her head. But she couldn't deny she'd been very much aware of Dalton taking up space in her office. "He was giving me some security tips."

"Right," Heather said with a grin. "We'll go with that."

Josie didn't want to have this conversation. "Back to work," she said on a gentle note. "I'll tell the others about our meeting."

She dreaded telling them anything, but she couldn't keep this from her employees. She only prayed she didn't have to shut this place down because of some lunatic.

Dalton drove around the neighborhood and searched for any signs that might give him a hint of what was going on. These older homes along the main thoroughfare aptly called Desert Valley Road had mostly all been turned into commercial businesses, such as the Desert Valley Medical Clinic where Officer Whitney Godwin Evans's husband, David, used to work.

Dalton was only in Desert Valley because of the K-9 training program he'd completed and his offer to work for the DVPD until after the holidays. But Desert Valley wasn't such a bad place to be. There were good people here.

He thought of Josie Callahan and stifled the surge that shot through his heart. Again, he had that feeling of awareness that he'd gotten the first time he'd met her. She'd been holding a tiny infant while she reassured the baby's frantic mother that she'd take good care of her baby boy.

He'd been smitten with her from the beginning, but he'd tried to squelch those erratic feelings. Maisy needed him, and he wasn't always home to help her. That's why he'd been so glad to find a day care that allowed older children to attend the after-school and late-shift programs. He didn't want anything to jeopardize that arrangement.

And he sure didn't want any harm to come to the children or Josie and her staff. So he cruised the neighborhood around the day care, located near the town center. The streets were quiet, the modest homes clean and settled.

Then he glanced at a rutted dirt lane that led to a run-down house sitting like a squatter in a rocky, isolated corner lot.

A dark, older-model car was parked at an angle by the house.

It looked like the car he'd noticed driving away from Josie's house last night.

"Let's go investigate," Dalton said to Luna. She woofed her agreement from the backseat.

Dalton wondered if Josie's tormentor could be hiding in plain sight.

FIVE

"This isn't easy," Josie said a few hours later.

She had the whole staff gathered in the break room. Her aunt, whom she'd already told everything, was sitting in the front lobby with the last of the children. Maisy was there with Aunt Marilyn, helping out as usual.

Glancing at the clock, she said, "I hoped Officer West would be able to help me explain this but...you know how it goes with police officers."

Heather's grin brightened, but she wiped her face clean when Josie didn't grin back. Josie had to tell them what was going on to keep them safe and to show them that she wasn't hanging out with Dalton West because she suddenly had a hankering to date a K-9 cop. Not that the notion hadn't entered her mind.

"What is it?" Tricia Munson asked, her brown eyes full of anxiety. "Are you laying some of us off already? Is that why you called me in for this meeting?"

"It's not that," Josie said, sinking down on a chair. "I've received some threatening notes."

"What?" Heather's blankness vanished. "Is that why you've been so preoccupied?"

"Yes," Josie said. "Officer West found one of the notes on the playground yesterday after someone tried to open the back door."

They all started mumbling among themselves.

"Listen, let me finish," Josie said. "I've talked to Aunt Marilyn about this already, but I need you to understand—this might be nothing. I received another note today." She glanced at Heather. "The package you found at the door."

Heather gasped. "I'm so sorry. I had no idea."

"It's not your fault," Josie replied. "We don't know if it's a joke or if it's an upset parent trying to scare me. Or maybe someone else."

"That granny woman sure wasn't happy with anybody in Desert Valley," Floyd, the maintenance man, said. "Could it be her pulling some strings from jail?"

"You mean Patrick Murphy's grandmother, Alice Shepherd?" Tricia asked. "They arrested her after she tried to take Patrick. Surely she isn't starting all over again? She'd be crazy to do that."

Floyd let out a grunt. "I rest my case."

Thinking she needed to school her staff on being sensitive to others' suffering, Josie hadn't even considered Floyd's suggestion. "Mrs. Shepherd is being treated for her mental problems, so I don't think this is coming from her. But I'll mention it to Officer West."

She took a sip of water. "We don't want to scare our parents, but they'll need to know if it keeps happening. Before we alert them, however, you need to keep this among the staff. Officer West wants to check on every parent who has a child here to rule out that possibility. So he might have to interview all of us."

"Does he think it's one of them? Or one of us?" Tricia asked.

"No. He's not accusing anyone. We're being diligent in making sure we've covered every possibility. It could be kids playing pranks."

"Are the notes threatening?" Floyd asked.

"Not in an obvious way," Josie said.

"Can we see them?" another worker asked.

"No. Officer West filed them as evidence, and he's filled out an incident report." Josie stood, ready to end this. "Remember, they've only come to me. No one else is being threatened in a direct way. I've alerted the police, and Officer West is on the case since his daughter attends the after-school program here. Several officers place their children in our care, so the whole department will be aware. He's putting a patrol on the street during the workday and after hours. And if I can find some money in the budget, I might put in a security system."

"I know a guy," Floyd said, coming over to pat her on the arm. "We're all behind you, Josie."

"Thank you, Floyd," she told the older man who seemed like everyone's grandfather. He'd retired from coaching soccer at the high school, and she was blessed to have him. "We're going to be okay, I promise."

But even as she said it, Josie didn't know how she could make such a promise. She'd pray her way through this situation. And hope that Dalton found something soon.

Nothing. He'd found nothing.

The old house was vacant and falling down, and the car looked like it'd been stripped for parts. But Luna had displayed a keen interest in the car. Since they hadn't found any items near the automobile or in the trunk, he couldn't be sure if she'd sniffed something she recognized or if she'd had a false alert from too many squirrels hanging around.

The house was locked, so he didn't search inside. But the place gave him a feeling he didn't like. He'd have to keep an eye on it.

With nothing concrete to connect this place or the abandoned car to the case, he had to move on. But he would alert the chief.

After taking care of that, he headed back to the day care and saw Josie's aunt Marilyn with a cluster of children.

"Daddy," Maisy said, waving. "We're reading. Miss Josie is having a meeting. Can I finish this story?"

He nodded. "Good idea, honey. I need to see Miss Josie, anyway."

Marilyn Carter nodded at him. "They're in the break room."

Dalton hurried back, Luna by his side.

When he walked into the room, several workers were gathered around Josie. "Did I miss the meeting?" he asked.

Josie looked relieved. "We just finished. I waited but…they were anxious to hear what was going on."

Dalton nodded to the half-dozen workers. "I'm sorry I'm late. I'm sure Josie has explained, but if you have any questions—"

Everyone starting talking at once, so Dalton tried to calm all of them, one question at a time. And then he asked them some questions of his own.

An hour later, Josie locked up and turned to Dalton. "You can't keep escorting me home."

"I don't mind," he said, his gaze moving over her in that way that left her both warm and chilled. "Part of the job."

And he was all about doing his job, she reminded herself. She shouldn't read anything else into this. He needed the extra training with his partner, Luna, and what better way than to find out who was harassing her?

But her need to remain independent kicked in. "I can make it home. It's not that far."

"It's getting dark," he said. "Don't waste time arguing."

"Right." He wanted to get on with his day, too. *Stubborn, meet stubborn.* "Let's go."

"Are you eating with us again, Miss Josie?" Maisy asked from the patrol car, hope in her question.

"No, honey. Your daddy's being a gentleman and making sure I get home okay."

Maisy shrugged and gave her father a disappointed glare. "Why can't she have dinner with us?"

Dalton looked heavenward and then tried to explain. "Because we have our house chores and homework, and Miss Josie is tired and she wants to go home to her house, alone."

"Alone isn't fun," Maisy said with a pout.

"She has a point," Dalton said to Josie.

"But we can't do this," Josie whispered to him. "She might get the wrong idea."

"I know." He did the visual thing, his sharp gaze roaming the street. "It's kind of out of the blue, but I wouldn't mind taking you out to dinner sometime."

Josie blinked. "Did you just ask me on a date?"

He looked sheepish. "Maybe when...things settle down. You know, as friends."

"You'll be gone after Christmas, Dalton. It can't happen. Even as friends."

Giving her a resigned stare, he said, "Right. Forget I asked." Whirling, he added in a gruff command, "Let's get you home safely."

Josie wished things could be different, but she hardly knew the man. Besides, she wanted to stay in Desert Valley, and Dalton planned to move back to Flagstaff.

But...he *had* asked. Probably felt bad that she was alone and being harassed. A shiver moved like a caught spiderweb against her skin. What did this person want from her?

She got in her car, her mind still on Dalton. But when she looked up and saw a red rose lying tucked into one of the windshield wipers, Josie jumped back out.

Parked across the lot, Dalton got out and hurried over. "What is it?"

She pointed to the rose.

His expression grim, Dalton took a pen out of his pocket and lifted the wilted flower from the wiper. It stood out in stark contrast against her white car.

"A card," he said, motioning to the cream-colored square attached to the flower. He flipped the card over.

'Tis the season. Soon, I'll be sending you something special.

"That's definitely a threat," Dalton said. "Josie, I think it's time we question everyone you know here."

Before she could answer, a shot rang out and Dalton tugged her down against the truck and shielded her as glass from her car's windshield exploded all around them.

Josie shook all the way home.

She kept glancing at Dalton. When they got to her place, he got out with Luna and Maisy at his side. He'd called for backup after someone had shot at her, but the police hadn't found anyone. The shooter had gotten away, and even though they'd scoured the parking lot, they hadn't found any bullets. Josie's car couldn't be driven until she had a new windshield.

"Do you think your aunt would mind if Maisy stays with her while I check your house?"

The girl stared her down. "Daddy told me you're getting an alarm system. I don't mind staying with Miss Marilyn. You need to be safe."

Amazed at Maisy's calm acceptance, Josie said, "You're so patient. A real trooper." The girl had barely flinched when Dalton had hurried to check on her after Josie's windshield had been shot out. But Luna barked incessantly, anxious to do her job.

"Comes with the territory," Maisy said in a mature tone. "Can Luna go with me?"

"I need Luna to work," Dalton said. "She's good at sniffing out trouble spots."

Josie tried to sound animated. "Did my aunt tell you about her dog? He's a tiny Chihuahua named Boo. You'll love him."

Maisy grinned. "I can hold him?"

"Sure." Josie's chuckle was ringed with a frazzled edge. "Let's walk over there."

"She has boys," Maisy pointed out, her nose in the air.

"True, they're not girls for you to play with, but they're fun kids," Josie replied, her gaze hitting on Dalton while she tried to keep things light for Maisy's sake. She noticed Dalton checking the immediate area to make sure no one was lying in wait.

Soon, she had Maisy settled with her aunt, the sound of boys boasting and little Boo barking giving her hope that her world wasn't about to cave in.

"Thank you," she mouthed to Marilyn. Her aunt nodded and held her hands together, prayer style. Her aunt was a good prayer warrior. "We'll talk later."

"Come over for dinner," Aunt Marilyn said. "And bring Dalton with you. We've got a big pot of stew going."

"Thanks," Josie said, thinking it wasn't such

a good idea to invite Dalton and Maisy for another meal.

Hurrying back to Dalton, she said, "Aunt Marilyn said we need to come and have dinner with them. No arguments, unless we find something we need to deal with."

His eyes centered on her. "We'll go over every inch of your house and yard. But before dinner, I need you to level with me about your past."

"The yard is clear," he told her a few minutes later.

Josie nodded. In her mind, she'd gone over all the details of her marriage, Douglas's death and the days following. Could that have something to do with this?

"I'll check the bedrooms," he said as they headed inside her house.

Full official mode. He wouldn't take no for an answer, but she wasn't sure what he expected her to say. That her past had finally caught up with her? That her life in Texas had not been a pleasant one?

"All clear," he said when he came back.

She turned on the Christmas-tree lights. "It doesn't feel like a holiday around here."

"Someone threatening you can certainly ruin the joy."

"I won't let them do that," she replied on a determined note. "I've worked too hard for this."

He crowded the small space with a comforting presence that made her feel safe. "Then you'd better tell me why you had to start over here in the first place."

He ordered Luna to heel, and then he walked into the kitchen. And immediately filled it with enough man power to make her want to shrink back.

But she held her ground. "I won't let you steal my joy, either."

"I have to know everything about you so I can figure this out," he said, his eyes moving over her face like a laser. "It's standard procedure. And it could save your life."

He was right. Instead of being aggravated, she should be thankful. She handed him a cup of coffee and then said, "My husband's family resented me even before he died. I was never good enough for them, and I didn't produce grandchildren right away, so they pretty much treated me like the enemy. And after his death, they blamed me for him being distracted the day of the accident. Somehow, they knew we'd had a bad fight that morning before he left for work. After he died, I received a large amount of life insurance money, which my mother-in-law seemed to think I should share with her."

Dalton's eyes held hers in a way that stripped her soul.

"Enough money for one of them to come after you?"

"More than enough," she said in a low whisper. "But I didn't tell them I was coming here. I sold most of my belongings and I left. No one back there could possibly know where I am now."

He gave her a sympathetic stare. "Josie, finding a person is easy with the available technology these days. They might have put a GPS on your car or phone. Or someone could have seen you leaving and tipped them off. If they know you have a relative here, it'd be the first place they'd look."

"I tried to be careful," she said. "I never dreamed someone might come after me. But... no matter who's doing this, we have to stop them."

"We'll keep working on it," Dalton replied. "Sooner or later, they'll either slip up or we'll get a solid lead."

Placing her coffee cup on the counter, she asked, "Dalton, what if it is one of my in-laws? What if they've found me?"

SIX

Dalton tried to be honest. "I can't say for sure until I do some investigating, but they're on the list. Why would they come after you in such a strange way? Cryptic notes, and now shooting at you? Why wouldn't they show up at your door and tell you what they want?"

She finished her coffee and put her cup in the sink. "After we got married, Douglas changed. He became moody and mean, and nothing I did pleased him. I soon figured out he'd married me so he'd have someone to wait on him and pamper him the way his mother did. They blamed me for his bad moods and spread it around that they didn't like that their son married a girl from the trailer park."

Casting her gaze downward, she said, "My mother worked as a maid at the local hotel. She wasn't the best mother ever, and she died not long after I got married. My father left when I was a baby. So I was pretty much a pushover. I wanted to please everyone, but I always failed."

Dalton's heart burned with anger. This kind, gentle woman had been through a lot more than he'd imagined. "So do you blame yourself for your marriage going bad?"

"I did at first. But I grew stronger as I matured. Going to church helped with that. Aunt Marilyn helped me, too. She'd come and visit and bring me things. I owe her a lot."

She lifted her head up as if to shake away the bad memories. "Anyway, that's my past and so here we are."

"Tell me a little more about your in-laws," he said, wishing he could wipe away the sadness in her eyes.

"While they weren't rich, my in-laws were straitlaced pillars of the community. My father-in-law worked in upper management at the refinery, and he got Douglas a job there after Douglas quit college. Douglas Senior passed away a few months after Douglas died. Janine, my mother-in-law, kept saying Douglas's death had killed her husband, too. My father-in-law was never the same after Douglas died. They quit speaking to me."

"You mentioned more than one in-law. Any other children?"

"Yes. My brother-in-law, Randall, is estranged from his mother now, but he and Douglas stayed close. He was pretty upset when Douglas was killed in that accident. He hated the refinery and refused to work there. He studied to become an electrician, but I don't know if he ever finished school. He worked for a cable company last I heard."

She shook her head. "He pretty much kept to himself, and he had a girlfriend who kept him busy, but right before I left they got married and moved to Louisiana." She wiped at a speck on the counter. "Janine was all alone and she didn't have a lot of money, and she suddenly decided I should share the money I'd received with her."

"Did you?"

"I gave Janine some money, but I explained to her I wanted to use the rest to start my own day care. I'd worked in child care since high school, so I could pay for college, course by course, through the years until I finally got my degree. She laughed at me and told me I'd never succeed."

He watched her face, wondering if one of her in-laws might have come looking for her. But money could bring out the worst in people. "Did *they* ever threaten you before?"

"No." Then she paused. "But…after Douglas's death, she turned on me. They didn't like me, anyway. After he died, his parents seemed to shift into true hatred for me. They implied if I'd been a better wife, Douglas might still be alive. Then when Douglas Senior had a heart attack,

Janine poured out her angst on me. She believed the stress of her son's death contributed to my father-in-law's death. And I think she was right."

She inhaled a shaky breath. "She started spreading rumors about me. I quit my job, since my boss kept hearing the rumors and questioned me daily. I knew what would happen next. I'd be fired for not being a fit child care provider. So I took the easy way out. I left." She looked into Dalton's eyes. "I came here with a clean record, and I'd like to keep it that way."

"But you mentioned the insurance money."

"His father never knew about it," she said. "I was so shocked that Douglas had taken out a policy and left it to me that I didn't tell anyone for weeks. But after his dad died, I went to Janine and blurted it out. That's when things got ugly. Janine demanded that I turn over the money to her. Told me she was broke, and that Douglas Senior hadn't left her much of anything."

Dalton saw the apprehension in her eyes.

"I've never seen anyone so angry," she said. "I know she was hurting. She'd lost her son and her husband in a matter of months."

"So you gave her money to appease her?"

She looked surprised and then resolved. "I gave her part of the money, but I'd had enough of Texas and the family, so after I talked to Aunt Marilyn she suggested I should come here for a while. When she told me she'd help me start a day care,

I jumped at the chance." She wiped at her eyes. "And here I am. I've been here getting the day care up and running. Why would they wait so long to confront me?"

"They found a way to track you," Dalton said. "But the notes and even being shot at could be coming from a man or a woman. The brother maybe, if she put him up to it."

She started around him, her frown full of doubt. "I don't think it's either of them. My mother-in-law is frail and sickly, so I can't see her doing it," she said. "Randall's trying to improve his life, so why would he try something like this?"

Dalton touched a hand to her arm. "Josie, people who are desperate will do anything, especially when it involves money. Your mother-in-law might be frail and unable to travel, but she could have sent someone to find you."

"And what will they do? Kill me and try to get what's left in my bank account? They can't do that."

"No, but they could take you and force you to get the money out of the bank and then kill you. Is there any of the money left?"

Ignoring the crouching fear his words provoked, she said, "I have a small savings account and a modest checking account. My aunt and uncle cosigned on the loan and put up a share of the front money. They did that to protect me and because they own some other real estate, including this house."

Dalton could see how much she had riding on this venture. "Maybe they're threatening you, thinking you'll leave and go back to Texas. Then they could work on getting their hands on what they consider to be a fortune."

"Or maybe they want to torment me." She stopped and gasped, her fingers digging into his shirtsleeve. "Dalton, that has to be it. If they keep at this, the parents will remove their children from the day care. I could lose everything. What if this *isn't* about getting to the money? What if they want to ruin me?"

An hour later, Josie sat with her aunt and uncle in their den. The boys and Maisy were in another part of the house, watching a movie. They'd had a quiet dinner, but Josie could barely eat.

"I'm sorry," she said now. "I can't believe this is happening."

"Now don't go jumping ahead," her uncle Jack said. "Let Dalton do his job."

"He's right, honey," Marilyn said. "This doesn't mean someone is out to do you in. I know your life with Douglas was hard, but he's gone now. He can't hurt you anymore. Nor can his mama or his brother. We're not gonna let that happen."

Josie whirled from her aunt to Dalton. "Douglas was cruel and irrational, and he didn't trust me at all. Our marriage was over long before he died. I just didn't have the courage to leave him."

"Did he abuse you?" Dalton asked, an edge in his voice that made her uncle sit up and take notice.

"No," she said. "He didn't love me. He drank too much and flirted with other women and complained about his job. He was careless and cynical and...he didn't trust anyone. And because of that, I cowered and became some kind of passive person that I didn't even recognize."

"But you're okay," he reminded her, the admiration in his eyes warming her. "You're doing great. Use your strength to keep your head clear. We've had three messages and now a near-shooting, so this is serious. And it'll probably get worse. You told me you'd changed, and I believe you."

"She sure has changed," Marilyn said with a chuckle, her dark curls bobbing around her face. "She stared down contractors and inspectors and town council members to get our business up and running, and she worked hard on finding a good team to take care of our children. I'm very proud of her and I know if my sister was alive, she'd be proud of her, too."

"Thank you, Aunt Marilyn," Josie said, touched. "But don't sing my praises too much. I'm so worried right now I don't think I'll be worth much come morning. My focus is on the day care and the children."

"Why don't you stay with us tonight?" her aunt asked. "We have plenty of room."

Josie shook her head. "No. I'll be okay. My house isn't that big, and I've got locks on all the windows and doors, thanks to my wonderful landlord." She smiled at her uncle. "Now, I need to get home and I'm sure Dalton feels the same way."

"I don't mind," he said, standing. "But Maisy does have school tomorrow, and it's party day. She'll be wired when she gets home."

"Oh, that's right," Marilyn said. "School's out for the Christmas break. We'll be busy with extra kids all next week."

"I'll go get Maisy for you," Jack said. Then he turned and gave Dalton a serious appraisal. "If you ever need to bring Maisy to us, she's welcome here. We have a room that's all girl—Marilyn's getaway room. It's like a spa and a boutique all rolled up in one—as my wife likes to say. Maisy viewed it earlier tonight, so I know she'd be comfortable there."

"Thank you," Dalton said, appreciation in his eyes. "It's good to know she's got people like you to look after her." Then he looked at Josie. "And I'm glad you have these two next door."

"All the more reason to be extra-careful," Josie replied after her uncle went down the long hallway to the other wing of the house. "We have to take care of Maisy and the other children, first and foremost. I was looking forward to our party for the kids next week and then the couple of days we'll have off during Christmas."

"You can still look forward to this special time of year," Marilyn said as they walked to the door. "We're gonna have faith and get through this. God led you here so He's not gonna abandon you now."

Josie wanted to believe that with all her heart. But after Dalton and Maisy escorted her home, she couldn't shake the sense of dread.

Dalton checked the house again, Luna already learning the routine. "I'll do a sweep of the yard, front and back, before I leave," he told her. "Make sure you're locked in tight." Then he handed her a card. "Call me if you see or hear anything that scares you."

He scared her. The way he cared about her safety was a whole new experience for Josie. No man had ever tried so hard to show her that he wanted to protect her, and this man barely knew her. His kindness was so overwhelming that she wanted to push him away and tell him that she didn't deserve his protection.

But her aunt would shun that notion. She'd always been Josie's champion, even when her own mother hadn't encouraged her. No wonder Josie had married a bully of a man who treated her like a doormat. She'd cowered from her bitter mother for years. But after counseling at church and being with people who encouraged her, she wasn't a doormat anymore. She'd learned that she could fight for herself and still come out on the other side. Unlike her mother, who'd never found the strength to get on with her life after Josie's father had left.

She'd fight now. But she'd fight smart. "I promise I'll keep my phone on my pillow," she told Dalton. "I'll leave lights on and I won't go outside. If I do, I'll call my uncle. And… I did take some self-defense crash courses after Douglas died."

"All of that is good," Dalton said. "Still, be careful."

"I will," she said.

He checked the yard and came back for Maisy. "Let's get you home, Ladybug."

Josie smiled at the endearment. But Maisy looked up at her with big, solemn eyes. "You could come and stay with us, Miss Josie."

Josie heard the catch in the girl's suggestion. Maisy was putting on that brave front. Even though they'd tried so hard to shield her from what was really going on, the kid had a keen intuition.

But Maisy also had enough sense to know this was about more than beefing up security.

She hated putting this child through any more trauma. Her eyes met Dalton's, sympathy piercing her heart. "That's so sweet of you, Maisy. But I have everything I need right here. You don't have to worry. Your dad has coached me on what I need to do. He's being very smart, practicing on me and letting Luna get in some practice, too."

Maisy glanced at her daddy. "Sometimes, even things we've practiced can still get messed up."

Dalton's frown ripped at Josie's consciousness. "Maisy, what do you mean by that, honey?"

Maisy's stoic expression turned to cautious. "Nothing. But…people get hurt all the time. Sometimes, you can't protect them."

Dalton's tanned skin turned pale. "You're right. But we can't stop trying. And I'm going to do my best to protect you and Miss Josie and everyone else around here."

"I don't want to leave here," Maisy said. "I like living here. I don't like Flagstaff."

Realization clutched at Josie and she saw the resolve in Dalton's eyes, too. "But we talked about this," he said, his tone soft. "We'll find a nice new neighborhood and start fresh with Luna. She'll watch out for us."

Luna's ears pricked up, and she gave Maisy a loving stare, as if she knew exactly what the little girl was feeling. Which she probably did.

"I don't like it there," Maisy said. Then she rushed to Josie and hugged her close. "I like it here better."

Dalton's jaw clenched. Josie could see the pain in his stormy gray eyes. "We'll talk about this later, okay? We have to get home right now."

Josie hugged Maisy close and told her she'd see her tomorrow. "Remember, I need you to help me pass out cookies and Christmas ornaments."

Maisy smiled at that. "Okay."

But Dalton wasn't smiling. He nodded and turned with a stiff back and hurried his daughter to the car.

Josie had never felt so alone.

And she'd never seen such hurt in a man's eyes. Maisy's heartfelt pleas had broken him in two.

Dalton West carried a lot of burdens on his broad shoulders. And now, he'd added her to that load.

She hoped this would end soon. They could all use a break. But her instincts told her this was just the beginning.

SEVEN

Dalton checked in with Josie the next afternoon when he picked up Maisy. He hoped she'd had a safe, restful night. He'd wanted to call her and offer to give her a ride to work, but he'd decided that could come across as unprofessional. Besides, she had already planned to ride to work with her aunt. So he waited all day and hoped he'd see her.

He found Josie in the nursery, holding a toddler against her shoulder while she rocked in a big comfortable chair. The sight of her sitting there with a child in her arms caused him to imagine things he had no business thinking about. Sure, he'd known her for months now, but he hadn't really *known* her until this week when they'd been forced together by some kind of sick person's handiwork.

He'd been smitten with her from the start, but Dalton had ignored those little tremors of attraction. Now, he couldn't deny that he liked Josie Callahan a lot. But...where could that admission take him? She was building a life here, and he wanted to go back to Flagstaff where Maisy could be surrounded by family. His mother kept calling and asking if they were coming home for Christmas.

Watching Josie right now, he didn't want to go anywhere. When she glanced up and saw him leaning against the doorjamb, her smile went wide and his heart went flip-flop.

"Hi," he said, crossing his arms against his chest. "He's a cutie."

She nodded and carefully stood, her hands holding the chunky little boy across his back. "He played himself out. His mom's on her way."

After putting the sleeping toddler in one of the cribs lined up along the room, she turned to Dalton and motioned to the wide hallway.

"How are you?" he asked, not knowing what else to say.

"Okay. Nothing happened last night. I didn't sleep very well, and I kept getting up to check the windows. I haven't seen any notes today, either. Do you think they could have given up?"

Dalton doubted that. "No, I think they're retreating because they've seen us together."

Her crestfallen face said it all. "I'd hoped…"

"I know," he said quietly, since her staff seemed intent on listening. "But you still need to be careful and stay aware. For now, you made it through today."

"We did," she said, her smile unsure. "We had

a great day with all the kids, and tonight we're all meeting at my aunt's house for a staff party. You're welcome to stop by."

Surprised and tempted, he said, "But I'm not on staff."

"You almost are," she said. "You seem to have assigned yourself as my personal bodyguard."

"Tired of me already?"

She blushed a becoming pink. "I didn't say that. But you do have a life, and I'm sure you don't need me in it."

"You might be wrong about that," he said, surprising both of them.

She stood there, her green eyes shimmering while she stared at him. Dalton felt a sizzle that reminded him of heat lightning moving over the desert. His mind filled with something sweet and right and welcome.

And then a preschooler running down the hallway screamed, and the moment was gone. Josie looked away and grabbed the escaping, giggling bundle of energy and lifted him up with a smile and a "Whoa!"

Whoa was right. Dalton had to gather his thoughts, so he turned to go find Maisy. Best if he got out of here right now. As long as Josie was safe, he could relax.

But…he'd never forget that moment that had just happened.

Lightning had hit him, and now a monsoon of

emotion was pouring through what had been the dry gully of his soul. And he had to wonder— *Is this what it feels like when God touches your heart with hope?*

Josie headed to her aunt's car. Her uncle had picked up Marilyn earlier, since they had some shopping to do. A lot of parents would need to work right up to Christmas, so they'd have a big group of children early next week, and then she'd have four days to celebrate with her family.

Thankful that her aunt and uncle had taken her in and helped her so much, she looked forward to a big Christmas dinner. Praying that she'd have that without any threatening letters or any more gunshots, she let out a breath. When her cell rang, she absently picked it up.

"Hello?"

Nothing.

"Hello?" Josie said again, her eyes on the traffic light, which glowed red.

Nothing. But she heard breathing.

"Who is this?" she asked, her heart rate speeding up. When the light turned green, she eased through the intersection.

The caller ended the call and her phone beeped.

By the time she pulled into her driveway, Josie had talked herself into believing the call had been a wrong number. Calming her jitters, she got ready for the party next door, and then she gathered the casserole she'd made and hurried to greet her coworkers.

But an hour later, after two more voiceless calls, she knew her tormentor had moved one step closer to her. Somehow, this person had found her cell number.

Dalton checked in with the patrol officer the chief had authorized to cruise the block surrounding Josie's house. So far, nothing was out of the ordinary. He believed the patrolman, but Dalton couldn't help but worry about Josie.

She should be at her aunt's staff party right now. The party she'd invited him to attend. He wasn't going, of course.

Dalton sat in the tiny apartment he'd rented three months ago, wondering if he'd made the right decision switching from detective to the K-9 unit. His chief back in Flagstaff had encouraged him to try something new after his wife had been killed.

Might help you to heal, Dalton. K-9s are not only good partners and officers, but they provide companionship. Both you and Maisy could benefit from that."

The chief had been right. Maisy had taken to Luna the first time he'd been allowed to bring the dog home. Now he couldn't imagine not having Luna around. She was smart, quick and she protected Maisy without question. He trusted the pound puppy that had been trained from a young age with his life.

But had he done the right thing, bringing Maisy here?

He watched his daughter now. They'd had a quick supper of soup and sandwiches, and now she sat staring up at the meager Christmas tree.

His heart hurting for her, he looked up from the paper he'd been trying to read and asked, "Hey, Ladybug, what do you think? Did we do okay on the tree?"

"It's really pretty, Daddy," she replied, Luna by her side. "But it's sure tiny." Then she glanced back. "Remember that big one you brought home, and we had to cut it over and over so it would fit by the fireplace. Mom and I laughed at you about that."

Dalton swallowed the emotions welling up inside him. "I do remember. What? About three years ago? But we got that tree down to size, didn't we?"

She nodded, her hand touching Luna's sleek fur. "That was the best time."

Dalton got up and went to sit on the floor beside her, his gaze on the few presents he'd managed to get wrapped. "Honey, I wish I could give you a big tree this year. But once we're back home, I'll buy you the prettiest tree we can find."

Maisy turned to stare up at him. "It's okay. I don't mind a little tree if we can stay here."

Dalton had been afraid that topic would resurface. "Honey, we've talked about this. I need to get back to Flagstaff so Luna and I can do our jobs."

"But why can't you do that here?"

Dalton tugged at one of her trailing curls. "Well, the Desert Valley Police Department isn't as big as the one in Flagstaff. We train here, and then we're sent out all over the state."

"Could you work close to here?" she asked. "That way we could stay?"

Dalton hadn't considered that. "I don't know. That depends on a lot of things. Why do you want to stay here so much?"

He thought he knew the answer, but he prayed she'd open up to him, anyway.

She pushed at her hair and swiped a hand across her nose. "I like it here. I like going to the day care 'cause Miss Josie and Miss Marilyn let me help out."

"And you're good at helping," Dalton replied, watching her for any changes in her expression or mood. "But you don't have to take care of everyone."

Bobbing her head, she said, "I don't mind. I need to make sure they're all safe."

"Is this about Patrick?" Dalton asked. "Because he's safe now and he's improving every day."

"But...we almost lost him."

Dalton motioned to her, and she scooted into his arms. "I know it's scary sometimes, what I do.

And… I can't promise I'll be able to save everyone who needs my help. But you know I'll give it my best shot, right?"

She nodded again. Then she looked up at him with big, misty eyes. "We couldn't save Mommy."

Dalton took in a breath, his lungs burning with a scorching heat. "I know," he said, kissing the top of her head. "I'm so sorry."

Maisy stared up at him, and then she pulled away. "No, you don't understand. I didn't save her, either." Then she got up and ran to her bedroom and slammed the door.

Dalton was headed after her when his cell buzzed.

Josie.

He stared at his daughter's shut door.

Then he answered the call.

"Dalton West."

"I hope I'm not calling at a bad time," Josie said, her tone hesitant.

"Uh… I do need to check on Maisy, but I can talk for a minute."

"Someone is calling my cell and then dropping the calls."

"You mean, hanging up?"

"Yes. They don't speak. They just…breathe."

He kept an eye on Maisy's bedroom door. "Do you want me to come over?"

"No. But you can add that to the police report.

It has to be the same person who left me those notes and the rose."

"And shot out your windshield." He walked toward Maisy's door. "Where are you now?"

"I'm at my aunt's house. The party is winding down, and I'm about to go home."

"Ask your uncle to go with you."

"I will. Just wanted to let you know." Then she said, "Dalton, are you okay?"

Could she read him that well already?

"Not really," he said. "I need to go check on Maisy. She's having a bad night."

"Go," Josie said. "I'm fine. We'll talk later."

"Can I call you once I get Maisy settled?"

"Yes," she said. "I'd appreciate that." Then she added, "I'm sending a little prayer for both of you."

"Thanks," he said. "I think we'll need that now more than ever."

An hour later, Josie's cell buzzed again.

She let out a held breath when she saw it was Dalton. "Hello," she said, sinking onto the couch. She had every light in the house on and all the outside lights shining into the front and back yards.

"Hi," he said, his voice sounding weary. "Any more calls?"

"No." She shivered in spite of the heater blasting through the overhead vents. "I hope they're done for the night. Or maybe forever."

"They have your private number now, so no, they're not done."

She detected irritation in his voice. "I realize that, Dalton. That's why I called you in the first place. Look, it's late and you sound tired—"

"No," he interrupted. "I'm sorry. It's Maisy. She's begging to stay in Desert Valley and I think… I think she's becoming too attached to the day care and…to you."

Surprised that he'd told her anything regarding his daughter, Josie shifted on the couch. "It's understandable after what you've both been through. She feels safe here, and she knows I will do my best to keep her safe when she's in my care."

"But what if you can't?" he blurted out.

So that was it? Josie's eyes burned with unshed tears for Maisy. "Are you saying you don't think the day care is safe now?"

She heard a rush of breath. "No, I'm not saying that. I'm not making any sense. She seems so overprotective of the younger children and I think—"

"She is overprotective," Josie replied before she could take it back. "She's afraid, Dalton. Because no one could save her mother."

"You mean, *I* couldn't save my wife," he said, his words gruff. "Is that what you're saying? Does Maisy talk to you about that?"

"She's made a few comments."

"You should have told me this sooner."

"I probably should have, but… I didn't want to upset you."

"She's my daughter. You can't keep things like that from me."

"No, that's not it," she replied, getting up to pace around the den. "Dalton, it's none of my business. I'm sorry. Look, you're obviously concerned about Maisy—"

A noise outside stopped her cold.

"But?" he said, as if he needed to hear her reasoning. "Josie?"

Another bump and then footsteps. "I think someone's in my yard."

"Listen, hang up and call 911. I can't leave Maisy, so I'm calling Whitney. She lives right around the corner. Okay?"

"Okay." She did as he said and listened to the silence of the house. A crash sounded somewhere outside, causing dogs to bark all along the street. A light went out in the backyard. Then she heard more footsteps, fast now. Hurrying. Another crash and the fence gate slamming shut. Were they coming around to the front of the house?

She stayed on the line with 911 and prayed her stalker wouldn't come inside her home.

EIGHT

Officer Whitney Godwin Evans circled back to the front of Josie's house, her K-9 partner, Hunter, moving ahead of her with a sure stride as the pointer did his job.

"They're gone," Whitney said, her gaze scanning the street.

"But someone was here?" Josie asked, wishing she hadn't scared the whole neighborhood.

Her uncle stood beside her while her aunt Marilyn stood on the porch of their house to make sure none of her rambunctious boys escaped to investigate on their own.

"Someone was definitely here," Whitney said, her blue eyes bright underneath the porch light. "Hunter sniffed all around the back fence and followed the trail to the front. They must have gotten in a car down the street."

"Did they do any damage?" Jack asked, his hand on Josie's shoulder.

Whitney pushed up her K-9 cap and lifted her

blond hair off her neck. "Broke out a security light and…left you a message."

Josie searched but didn't see anything in Whitney's hand. "Where it is? What did it say?"

Whitney gave her an apologetic stare. "They scrawled it on the back fence."

"What?" Jack moved closer to Josie.

"Can you show me?" she asked Whitney, dreading what she would see.

"Sure, but don't touch anything. We might find some trace evidence if we dust the fence for fingerprints. Or we could stumble on something in the grass and dirt back there."

She guided Josie and her uncle around to the backyard. "I'm having flashbacks of when this kind of thing happened to me here," Whitney said. "I thought I'd secured my yard but…people who want in can always find a way."

Jack grunted. "I think I'll sell the place. Too dangerous."

"I'm sorry," Josie said, wishing she hadn't brought this on her aunt and uncle.

"Do not apologize," Jack said, his tone soft. "You remember how you told us you were stronger now? Well, you have to stay that way, okay?"

She nodded, unable to speak. Whitney held up her flashlight so Josie could see the fence.

Scrawled in red, the message said, *You shouldn't be watching over anyone's children.*

Josie put a hand to her mouth. "They didn't come to steal from me. They came to shut me down."

"Who do you think it is?" Whitney asked, her solemn gaze moving over the bold letters and then back to Josie.

"I can't prove it," Josie replied, "but I'm beginning to suspect my in-laws. My father-in-law died right after my husband was killed. But my mother-in-law blamed both their deaths on me because my marriage was in trouble. My husband had one brother. Randall."

"Does he have a beef with you?" Whitney asked, in full interrogation mode now.

Josie cleared her throat. "I didn't think so, but now I'm wondering how far they'll go to ruin me. I left Texas to get away from my mother-in-law and her lies. But Randall and I always got along. He didn't like how I was being treated, but maybe she's convinced him otherwise. I can't see Janine physically capable of doing all this on her own."

"We've got help on the way," Whitney replied. "We'll do our best to figure it out."

Josie remembered Dalton's sharp words to her. He thought she was putting his daughter in danger. "Well, until we do figure it out, I think I should close down the day care."

"Honey, do you think that's wise?" Jack asked.

"I don't see what else I can do," she replied. "I don't want to scare the children or put them in danger."

Whitney touched a hand to her arm. "You've only got a couple of days next week, and a lot of parents are depending on you to be open—including me. If you stick to your routine, we might be able to nab this person."

"Or someone might get hurt. Or worse."

Whitney nodded. "Let me see if I can arrange things where one of us can be there for the two days you're open before the holidays. How's that?"

"That's not routine," Josie pointed out.

"No, but it might make them slip up," Whitney said. "Especially if they don't know we're there."

Josie could almost see the wheels turning inside Whitney's brain. "Well, several of you do have children in my care."

"That's right. They've probably been well aware of that, so they only strike when they think we're not around dropping off or picking up kids. We can change that up a bit."

"Be careful," Jack said.

"Always," Whitney replied. "Okay, we'll go over things here but…honestly, I doubt we'll get anything solid. From what Dalton's told us, they're covering their tracks. I'll call Dalton and give him a report. He'll be concerned."

Josie thanked Whitney and went next door with her uncle.

"You're staying with us until this is over," Marilyn insisted. "No arguments."

Josie didn't have the energy to argue. "Thank you," she said.

She wondered if Dalton would go along with Whitney's idea or if he'd pull Maisy out of the day care for good.

Dalton paced the floor, his phone in his hand. When it rang, he immediately answered Whitney's call. "Tell me."

"She's fine."

He listened while Whitney went over the details. Rubbing his forehead in an absentminded massage that wasn't really helping his developing headache, he said, "Thanks. I'll read over your incident report in the morning and file it with what I have so far. Still nothing on fingerprints or any other evidence from the day care, and I agree with you. Probably won't find anything since this person seems so thorough on covering his tracks."

"Hey, you might want to call Josie. She's thinking about shutting down the day care early for the holidays. She's worried about the kids."

Then she told him her idea.

"I did suggest that to her if things got worse," he replied, referring to putting an undercover officer inside the day care. "I can't be the one. I'm pretty sure whoever's behind all this has been watching and knows I've been on the case."

"They've seen all of us there," Whitney replied. "Sophie and Ryder, David and me. You. And Zoe and Sean. Actually, it's probably the best guarded day care in the state."

Dalton smiled at that. "You could be right. But one of us needs to be there 24/7 for the few days before Christmas. Or maybe all of us. Even if they see us. That kind of presence should scare them off or make them mess up."

Deciding they'd talk to Chief Hayes in the morning to get the go-ahead, Dalton ended the call.

Should he call Josie? He'd been harsh with her before because he was so upset about Maisy. He thought back to his big talk with Maisy. He'd knocked on his daughter's door and…she'd run straight into his arms.

"I'm sorry, Daddy."

"I'm sorry, too, honey. I know this is hard for you, but we have to stick together. You know I'd be lost without you, right?"

"And Luna," she added on a sniff. "She's my best friend."

Luna nudged at Maisy's hand, waiting for a response.

Maisy let go of Dalton and held tight to Luna.

Dalton agreed with her there. "Luna is the best. She watches over us and protects us and…she's why we came here."

"She's why I don't want to leave. If you take her to a big city, she might get injured." Maisy had looked up at him. "Sometimes police dogs get shot."

"Sometimes they do," Dalton replied. His job was easy compared to being a father. "Maisy, I can't promise you much in this life, but God watches over all of us."

"Was He watching over Mommy?"

Dalton gulped in a breath that bordered on a sob. A sob he'd long held tightly inside his heart. "I think He was. He watched and He cried because God hates evil. And the people who did this to your mother, to our family, they were the worst kind of evil. But God knew that no matter what those people did to your beautiful mother, He'd take care of her. And us. Honey, He took her home because someone evil took her life. And now your mommy is safe in His arms. He's watching over us and…we have to keep living. We have to hold out hope."

Maisy's face crumpled and her eyes filled with tears. "I did the right thing, Daddy. I called 911, but then they chased the car. And Mommy died in that wreck. If I hadn't called—"

Dalton's eyes filled with tears. "Oh, baby, is that what you think? That this is your fault?"

She bobbed her head, her sobs tearing at Dalton with an agony he didn't think possible. "I'm sorry. I'm trying to do better now. I help Miss Josie take care of the other children."

Dalton could see it all now, and his heart tore

into pieces for his sweet, smart daughter. "No, baby, I'm the one who's sorry. I should have realized this. You did the right thing, Maisy. You tried to help your mom. That dangerous man is the one who caused her death. Don't ever forget that."

He held her there and explained to her that she did nothing wrong. They'd both done their best. And then he tried to assure her that she didn't have to be a protector for everyone around her.

"But you are," Maisy pointed out.

"I guess I am," he replied, thinking the apple didn't fall far from the tree.

Finally Maisy lifted her head up to stare at him. "Miss Josie says God loves all of us. I hope He still loves me."

Dalton swallowed back the raw-edged emotion clogging his throat. "He does. He loves you and me and Luna, too. He even loved the people who hurt Mommy. But it's important that you and I always talk and work things out between us. God gives us that grace. He wants to help us, but He expects us to work hard on our own."

"He wants us to pray?"

"Yes," Dalton said, giving her a weak smile. "Prayer is how we talk to God."

"I talk to Mommy that way, too."

"That's good. So do I."

Then his amazing daughter said something he'd never expected. "I think Mommy would like Miss Josie."

Was that her way of asking for approval? Did his daughter want him to get involved with Josie Callahan? Maybe Maisy felt the same kind of guilt he did whenever he thought of having a woman like Josie in his life.

Or was she searching for someone to fill that deep void inside her heart, same as him?

After settling Maisy into bed with Luna in her own bed in the corner of Maisy's room, Dalton waited to hear from Josie.

He stopped pacing now. He and Maisy had crossed a threshold tonight, talking about her mother and God. He understood what his little girl was going through.

Thanking the Lord for that precious conversation, he found Josie's number on his phone. Time for another important conversation.

Josie hit at the pillow and turned over again. It was still early, but she'd told her aunt and uncle she was tired. Now she was in the attic room they'd converted into a nice guest bedroom complete with a small bath. Cozy and comfortable. She'd stayed in this room when she'd first arrived here. Aunt Marilyn kept it off-limits. This was the room she'd shown Maisy last night.

But in spite of the romantic, Victorian-inspired surroundings, Josie couldn't get comfortable.

Would she have to run again? Go somewhere else, far away. Why would Douglas's mother or brother come after her? Had she really been wrong not to hand over the insurance money her husband had left her?

Am I greedy, Lord? Josie prayed for clarity and guidance. She'd used the money to make a new start, and she'd given some to her church back home and the church here in Desert Valley. Other than the little bit she'd given to Janine, the rest was tucked away for a rainy day.

But someone wanted her destroyed.

Who could be that vindictive?

Her phone buzzed against the nightstand wood. Dalton's number came up.

"Hello," she said. "How are you?"

"I'm okay. I just wanted to check on you and tell you I'm sorry about carlier."

Letting that go, she said, "I can't sleep. Everything is such a mess, Dalton."

"I can't sleep, either," he said. And then he told her about his conversation with Maisy. After that, they talked for well over an hour about a lot of things, but Josie still wasn't sure if Dalton wanted Maisy around her right now. Or ever.

Dalton had just said good-night to Josie when a message from Chief Hayes flashed across his phone screen.

Possible lead on the day care case. Call me first thing tomorrow morning.

NINE

Bright and early the next morning, Dalton sat at his kitchen table reading the report about the car he'd discovered at the old run-down house not far from the day care. He'd asked the chief if one of the crime scene techs could check it out.

The chief had sent him the results after they'd talked on the phone this morning.

"So, I was right about that abandoned car?" he said after the chief told him what they'd found.

"Looks that way," Chief Hayes replied. "We didn't find any insurance or registration information on it. But one of the techs did find an old bill of sale underneath the seat. It was definitely purchased a month or so ago from a used-car lot off I-20 W near Lubbock, Texas. Cash."

"Texas." Dalton's gut burned. "Josie's from a small town near Waco. Pine Cone."

"Well, I think that's a pretty good lead," the chief replied. "That's about all we have, but if someone bought an old used car in a hurry and drove it from Texas to Arizona and then abandoned it, I'd say that person might be on a mission."

Dalton told the chief about Josie's in-laws. "Sounds like we might be on to something. Luna knew it, too. She alerted near the car, but I didn't find anything that was helpful. I'll do some digging around and maybe call the police in Pine Cone. I have a list of other possible suspects from that area, too."

"Careful with that," Chief Hayes warned. "If it's a small town and her in-laws were prominent, the locals won't want to divulge a lot of information."

"I'll keep that in mind," Dalton replied.

"We can't locate the owner of the abandoned house," the chief said. "And you didn't find anything?"

"No," Dalton replied. "Just dust and empty rooms. If anyone has been squatting there, they cleaned up after themselves."

"And left a car behind," Chief Hayes said before ending the call.

Dalton intended to do some work this morning. Being a rookie on short-time until after the holidays, he didn't have a desk to work from. He had to borrow from the department or work from home. Today was Saturday, and after his talk with Maisy last night, he wanted to stick close to her. Maybe do something fun.

But it was early and she was still asleep, so right now he'd see what he could dig up on the Callahan family from Pine Cone, Texas. Including the friends from Douglas Callahan's work place.

And he'd try to call Josie again.

But he wasn't quite sure what he'd say to her.

Josie stumbled downstairs and was greeted by her four wide-awake cousins. The boys ranged in age from five to ten and had more energy than a roadrunner on steroids.

"We want you to live with us forever," the youngest shouted as he launched himself against her. "We love you."

"I love you, too," Josie said, grinning against the headache that threatened to explode. "I need me some of your mama's good strong coffee."

"She's making pancakes and sausages," Ricky said.

Josie wondered if she'd be able to eat a bite. Her whole body ached from tossing and turning, and her eyes burned from lack of sleep.

Two of the boys whizzed by, loaded with electronic devices.

"They are so lame," Bryson, the oldest, said from his perch at the big kitchen island. He looked up at Josie with earnest eyes. "I like Maisy. She's cool."

That got Josie's attention. "Are you two friends?"

"I see her at school and…at the day care."

Josie tried not to show her interest. "She's a sweet little girl."

Bryson shrugged. "Yeah, she's okay."

He got up and headed for the den, nonchalance written all over his face.

"I think he has a crush on Maisy," Marilyn whispered as she handed Josie a cup of coffee. "How'd you sleep, honey?"

"Not so good," Josie replied. "I don't know what I'm going to do."

"If it's too much stress, it might be a good idea to cancel the party."

Josie had thought about this and prayed all night. "How can we risk the children's safety for a party? It wouldn't be right."

"Maybe the threats will stop," her aunt said. "They shot at you when you were with a police officer."

"But they wrote on the fence. Bold. And Dalton thinks they'll keep at it."

"You and Dalton—"

"Are just friends," Josie said, the coffee warming her insides. "He expects me to take good care of Maisy while she's at the day care, and based on a conversation we had last night, I'm afraid he thinks I can't do that now."

"I'm sure he's worried," Marilyn said. She dished up fluffy pancakes and dashed each with red and green candy sprinkles. "Boys, your breakfast is ready."

"Where's Daddy?" Andy asked as he slammed up onto a barstool.

"Checking on things at the garage before he comes back to take you all Christmas shopping."

Josie enjoyed the extra time with her cousins and nibbled on a pancake and had a bite of sausage. When her cell rang, she got up and gave her aunt an apologetic shrug. Then she hurried to the enclosed porch on the back of the sprawling house.

"Hi."

"Hi," Dalton said. "Listen, can we meet for coffee or something?"

She sighed and stared out at the backyard where her uncle Jack had built an impressive treehouse around a towering pine tree. Maybe if she and Dalton had a conversation away from everything and everyone, they'd be able to communicate regarding Maisy's well-being. She had to be sure.

"Where do you want to meet?"

"How about the Cactus Café? They have pretty good coffee."

"Okay, I'll meet you there in about half an hour."

When she turned, her aunt was standing in the doorway. "Dalton?"

"Yes. He wants to meet for coffee. To discuss things."

"Uh-huh. Well, that's good. Do you need a ride?"

"No. I'll take your car if you don't mind."

"Text me when you get there," Marilyn said. Then she heard a crash in the kitchen followed by "Mom's gonna be mad."

Marilyn groaned and hurried to check on her boys.

Josie's nerves tightened when she rode by the day care. Slowing, she checked the front for any signs of an intruder, but was relieved to see a police car sitting in the parking lot.

Then she checked her rearview mirror to make sure no one was following her. It was a cold wintry Saturday with light traffic. Safe so far.

When she pulled up to the Cactus Café, she saw Dalton and Luna waiting patiently by the older-model police car he'd been temporarily issued.

"Where's Maisy?" she asked when she got out of the car.

"A friend invited her to a Christmas party at the church, so she decided to go," he said. "So much for my plans to spend some quality time with her. But at least it gives me some time to talk to you privately right now."

She nodded, wondering what was coming. "I'm sure being with other kids her age at church will do her good," Josie said. Then she stopped short, a hand to her mouth. "And I told myself I wouldn't give unsolicited advice to you anymore."

He shook his head and glanced around the parking lot. "About that, I really am sorry…" Lifting away from his car, he added, "Last night was tough all the way around."

Feeling contrite for doubting him, she said, "Buy me a cup of coffee, Officer, and you can tell me all about it."

Relieved that Josie was willing to listen to his excuses for being so rude, Dalton found them a booth and ordered two coffees and a couple of cinnamon rolls. "You were right. Maisy is holding a lot of anxiety inside that brain of hers."

"I'm sorry," Josie said. "I was trying to help, and I made things worse."

"No, you opened my eyes to what was right in front of me. I know she's still grieving. We both are. But Maisy has it in her head that neither of us did enough to save her mother. Hard to swallow and really hard to explain to a child."

"I can't imagine how tough it must be. It's horrible to lose a loved one, but for a child to lose a parent, it must be a hundred times worse. I didn't want to interfere, and when she'd say something random to me, I thought if I listened to her, it would help."

"What exactly did she say to you?"

Josie took a sip of her coffee, her eyes full of sympathy.

"The other day while you were checking outside she said it was up to *her* to take care of *you*."

"Wow." Dalton's heart cracked a little more.

"That's a big responsibility for such a little girl. But it makes sense now that I know she felt responsible for her mother's death."

"Exactly." She took in a deep breath. "I wanted to talk to you about it, but all of these weird things keep happening and… I couldn't find the right time."

"And I'm too stubborn to listen to someone who's with my daughter practically every day. I'm sorry."

Her forgiving eyes gave him hope. "You have a lot on your mind, so don't apologize."

Dalton pointed to the cinnamon rolls. "Peace offering?" She smiled, and his heart rolled over and started a fast beat.

"I nibbled at a pancake at my aunt's house. I couldn't eat when I first got up, so now I'm hungry."

"Have at it," he said, relief washing over him.

"Now that we've settled that," she said between bites, "I want to hear if the chief's call had anything to do with my stalker. Whitney said she'd fill you in on last night's intruder."

"She did," he said. "I don't like it."

"What are you not telling me, Dalton?"

"Eat up," he said, amazed at her intuitive nature. "Let's enjoy this quiet time together before we step back into the fray."

He didn't want to ruin the moment with the information the chief had given him. He'd tell her about that later.

And he didn't want to tell her that he'd done a thorough search regarding her mother-in-law. A search that had revealed some very surprising news.

TEN

They walked around a trail that wound through a small park near the town center, the sun warm on their skin even with the frosty temperature. Bright lights twinkled on the lamp posts scattered throughout the walkway, and red bows adorned an open-air square pergola near a small man-made brook. A decorated tree sparkling with colorful lights completed the festive atmosphere.

Josie's mood had changed now that she understood what had happened last night. Maybe she'd been right to blurt out her concerns regarding Maisy, since it had forced Dalton to have that talk with his daughter.

But now, she was itching to find out what was going on in his mind. Something had him stewing.

"A storm is coming in the next few days," Dalton said, his hand light on Luna's leash. "We might get snow for Christmas."

Josie grinned and shot him a quick glance. "That would make Maisy happy."

He turned to stare at her. "And what would make you happy?"

Surprised at the intensity of that question, Josie drew back. "Honestly, right now I'd like to feel safe again. I thought I was building a good life here. I work hard, and I love what I do. I don't want to disappoint anyone, and I don't want to be forced to leave a place I've come to love."

He studied her, his eyes moving over her in a way that left her soul stripped of any facades. "You won't have to leave. I'll make sure of that."

"I hope *I* can make sure of that, too. I hope my reputation will hold through all of this."

He lifted her chin with his thumb. "So if everything were okay? I mean, if none of this was happening and I called you out of the blue to go to dinner, how would that make you feel?"

Josie stared up at him and saw the burning question in his gray eyes. Was he asking her permission to…take things to a new level between them? She wouldn't lie to him, so she took a deep breath and gathered her courage. "That would make me feel very happy, Officer West."

He leaned toward her, his expression full of determination and demand. The pines swayed in a soft wind, causing her blue scarf to lift and flow out around her shoulders. While the air around them was crisp, the warmth in his eyes made her feel safe and comfortable. Too comfortable. But the longing in her soul couldn't be denied.

Josie waited, wondering how his lips would feel on hers.

"And how would you feel if I told you I'd like to kiss you?"

Her whole system buzzed to life. "I… I…uh… think I'd like that, too."

He moved closer and touched his lips to hers in a sweet, slow exploration that made Josie blush all the way to her toes.

Satisfied, he stepped back and gave her a smile that sizzled her bootstraps. "Okay, then."

Regaining her momentum, she asked, "Are you finished…interrogating me?"

"Not quite, but it's a start."

He guided her, holding a hand on her elbow. "But now we can talk about your situation. I don't know who's sending you the threatening messages, but I can tell you one thing for sure, Josie. It's not your mother-in-law."

Dalton saw the shock registering on her face. Pointing to a bench, he guided her over and waited for her to sit down.

"What did you find out?" she asked, her hands twisting against her knit scarf. "And why didn't you lead with this?"

"First, I did a search and made some calls from home this morning and, second, we needed a break from all that." His gaze moved over her face and settled on her lips. "And I don't regret that decision."

She met his gaze, her expression full of apprehension and caution. "Okay. Go on."

"According to the people I talked to in Pine Cone this morning, your mother-in-law, Janine Callahan, had a stroke and she's been in an assisted living facility for at least six months."

Josie put a hand to her lips. "I had no idea. I didn't keep in touch."

Dalton nodded. "Understandable, but this means we can rule her out. She can barely speak, according to the woman I talked to in the sheriff's department."

"Did you tell this woman why you were calling?"

"I was discreet," he said. "I know what I'm doing."

Josie sank back on the bench. "Poor Janine."

"That leaves the brother. He moves around a lot. He's not in Louisiana, though."

"I can't see Randall going to all this trouble."

"Well, somebody is. I checked out your husband's coworkers, too. Two of them still work at the refinery and have solid alibis. The third one, Perry Wilcox, is no longer employed there. I'm still trying to locate him."

"Wow, you've sure been busy."

He stood. "Yep. I have to go and pick up Maisy. I'll walk you to your aunt's car." Offering her a hand, he held Luna's leash and waited for Josie to turn back toward the town center. "This was nice."

"Yes. And you were right. I needed some downtime." She gave him a serious look. "What do you recommend I do about the party? The children have been anticipating it for weeks, and the parents need me to be there while they finish up work and shopping before the holidays. But I don't want to endanger anyone."

Dalton thought about his conversation with Whitney.

"I'll clear it with the chief to have myself and some other officer on the premises for the next three days."

"You'd do that?"

He saw the hope in her eyes. "I'll make it happen. And I think I know a way." He reiterated what he and Whitney planned—keep a K-9 officer on the premises at least for the next few days. "I think you need to alert the parents that you've received some concerning mail. Reassure them that you'll have protection for the near future."

She stopped at the end of the path. "Thank you, Dalton. I've relied on your advice throughout this nightmare, and I'll never forget how you've helped me."

"Hey, it's my job," he said, but when he saw the disappointment in her eyes, he tugged her close. "And *you*, Josie. It's you, too." Deciding to lay it all on the line, he added, "I was worried about Maisy, but she loves you, and I think you've been a good influence over her. I was worried about work, but that will take care of itself. I was still grieving but…that won't bring back my wife. I need to move on with my life, and… I'd be crazy if I didn't let you know that… I'd like to have you in my life. We don't have to rush anything but we at least should…try."

He watched as tears misted in her eyes. "Are you sure about that, Dalton? You're not fixating on me, are you? You and Maisy have been through a lot. I need you to be sure. And we haven't even talked about you leaving after Christmas."

"I'm pretty sure," he said, knowing his heart. "I knew it the minute I met you. It's not a fix. It's real. I'd like to see what happens with us. I don't have to take the assignment in Flagstaff."

She looked awestruck. "Really? But how can you be so sure about me?"

"Really. You were holding a little newborn baby. I saw the tenderness in your expression."

"Dalton."

His name on her lips in that sweet way told him she felt the same. But he had to ask. "Are *you* sure?"

"I'm beginning to hope," she said. "But—"

"But we have to get past this thing and decide what happens next, right?"

"Right." She pulled away and glanced toward her car. "I hope we'll figure this out soon and then—"

She stopped and pointed. "Dalton."

The sweetness in her voice had changed to distress.

He turned and checked her car.

A flat tire on the front left side and a message scrawled in red on her windshield.

Sacrifices and burnt offerings.

Dalton let out a breath. "How did he manage this in broad daylight?"

Josie stood staring at her car. Then her words sent a chill rushing through Dalton.

"That's taken from Exodus. A sacrifice to the Lord, according to Moses."

The sound of gunshots hit the air. One, two, rapid and sure. Dalton tugged Josie to the ground and held his body over hers. "I think he's trying to make you the sacrifice," he said in Josie's ear, his gun drawn.

"Finally, somebody saw something," Dalton said as he got back inside his patrol car where Josie was waiting.

Thankfully, there *had* been a witness. A woman getting out of her car across from the restaurant had noticed the guy leaving the message, and she'd ducked down when he raised the rifle and started firing. Dalton had seen her watching after the patrol cars had zoomed in, and when he'd questioned her, she'd delivered a good description.

"And she got a good a glimpse of him driving away in a dark-colored sedan," Josie said.

"A man with a beard, skinny and wearing sunshades."

Josie kept staring out into the parking lot. "A man who managed to slash a tire and leave me another cryptic message. A man who obviously carries a big knife or something that can penetrate a tire and a gun that he knows how to use."

That concerned Dalton more than he wanted to let on. This person was getting closer with each act. And carrying yet another weapon that he could use on Josie.

"And he also left a can of spray paint that we're having analyzed. So we have a full report, and an eyewitness who caught him in the act and watched him drive away."

Josie got out of the car and tugged at her scarf. "But she didn't see the license plate number. And I don't know anyone who fits that description. Randall Callahan is hefty and short. It can't be him."

Dalton wanted to make her see how the evidence was stacking up. "She said skinny, not tall. Maybe Randall lost weight."

"But how can we prove it's him?"

"I'm running checks to find his last known location, and we'll go from there," Dalton said. "The rest is paperwork and making sure we have all the accurate information, which we do. I'm still trying to locate Perry Wilcox, too."

"Okay."

Dalton and a bystander had changed the flat tire and put on the spare. They'd searched around the slashed tire but hadn't produced any evidence. A team was searching the parking lot for anything they could send to ballistics. Dalton wasn't holding his breath on finding any DNA or prints. But Luna had alerted and followed the scent two parking spaces over, near a trash bin. She'd emitted the same low growl he'd witnessed when they'd found the old, abandoned car.

The suspect had waited until midmorning when the restaurant wasn't so crowded. But the town center buzzed with Christmas shoppers who were so involved in getting things done they'd probably never even noticed him. A quick spray of paint on the windshield and one quick duck in beside her car to cut into the tire. Then he'd waited for the right time to shoot, but he'd missed, thankfully. When Dalton thought of how close he'd come, he felt sick to his stomach.

"He's been watching you," Dalton told Josie on the way back to her aunt's house. He'd insisted on driving her home. He'd call a friend to give him and Luna a ride back to his car.

Josie stared straight ahead. "He had to have followed me this morning, somehow. And I checked and rechecked."

"It's a small town, Josie. All he had to do was see your car and give you time to make a turn or two."

"Which means I'm not safe anywhere," she said.

Dalton came around the car before she could bolt into the house. "Hey, listen. This is a huge break. He got too close and someone spotted him. We have a description of him and the woman saw him with a rifle. We know it's a male. He's gonna slip up, and then we'll have him."

"And how long do I have to wait for that, Dalton? How long do I put my life on hold or keep putting my kids in danger?"

"I'll be right here with you," Dalton said. "No matter what, Josie. We're in this together."

She stared up at him, defeat in her eyes. "I believe you, but... I don't know how much more of this I can take."

Dalton wanted to pull her into his arms and hold her tight.

Instead, he took her hand in his and guided her up to the porch. "Don't give up on me, Josie. Remember, no matter what."

ELEVEN

Later that day, Josie's cell buzzed.

Dalton. He'd promised he'd call her and check on her.

She sat on the love seat inside the enclosed sunporch at her aunt's house, trying to read a book. But she'd read the same paragraph about five times. The boys were in bed, and her aunt and uncle were in the den watching television.

After the harrowing morning, Josie helped her aunt wrap some presents and clean the house. But now her mind kept whirling between wanting to kiss Dalton again to wanting to give up and run away from her fears. And him.

"Hi," she said, the memory of their walk through the park helping her keep it together.

"Hi." He sounded breathless. He'd told her he liked to go for long runs sometimes.

"Have you been running?"

"Yeah, but not in the way you'd think. I've been running around all day following leads."

She held her breath, dreading what he might have found. "And?"

"And we've located your former brother-in-law."

Pushing her book out of her lap, Josie stood. "Where?"

"He's living in Utah. Near St. George."

Josie's nerve endings trembled a warning. "That's not that far from us, Dalton. And it can't be a coincidence."

"I know. About two hours at most. I don't have all the details, but I've alerted the authorities there, and they'll question him. Without any solid proof, they can't hold him, so we'll see if he confesses or not."

"What about the spray paint can?"

"It'll take a while to hear back from the state lab on that one. But if it's him, he's probably been coming back and forth, so we can find out what kind of vehicle he drives and put out an alert. If he shows up again, we'll nab him for questioning."

"Could this be over?"

"It could be," he said. "If the authorities there can locate him and question him, then we have something to work with."

"Thank you," she said, caught between relief and despair. "I hope it's not Randall, but if it isn't him, then the nightmare won't be over."

"We'll keep at it," he said. "Meantime, you go on with planning your big party for the kids.

You'll have plenty of K-9 officers patrolling next week, and they'll be at the party, too. I told the chief it would be a good PR move to teach the kids all about how we train our partners."

"You're something else, Officer West."

They talked a while longer and then ended on a high note. He told her he'd see her in church tomorrow.

Josie sat there in the dark and accepted what her heart already knew. She was falling for Dalton.

The next morning, Dalton hurried Maisy out the door to church. Feeling hopeful for the first time in a week or so, he smiled when they got in the car.

"We don't go to church much as my friends do," Maisy said, buckling her seat belt. "Are we going because Christmas is coming?"

"That and because you've been active in some of the church happenings, so I thought it was time I got more involved, too. I know I've missed a lot because of work but I'm going to do better."

Her grin said it all. "I'm glad, Daddy. All the other parents go with their kids."

Dalton silently kicked himself. "I'm sorry I didn't think about that, honey. Daddies get so busy sometimes they don't make the right decisions."

Maisy rolled her eyes. "And…some dads are afraid to go to church."

"You are way too smart for your own good," Dalton replied.

But she was right. He was already sweating just thinking about walking into a crowded sanctuary. He'd gone before only because of Maisy. Now he wanted to go for himself, too.

But after he parked the car and shook a few hands, the friendly atmosphere of the Desert Valley Community Church helped to calm Dalton. When Maisy poked him and pointed to where Josie sat with her relatives, his pulse quickened and he found his strength.

Time to turn back to God. And maybe it was time to forgive himself for not being able to save his wife.

About midway through the service, Dalton's cell buzzed. Discreetly checking his phone screen, he saw that the chief had called. Then a text.

Urgent. Found Randall Callahan.

Dalton waited until the service was over and then leaned close to Josie. "I have to go. Can you take Maisy with you to your aunt's?"

She nodded, alarm clouding her face.

He'd have to explain later, so he whispered to Maisy that he had to go to work, so she'd be going with Miss Josie. Maisy bobbed her head and smiled up at Josie.

At least he didn't have to worry about her while he headed to the police station.

"Randall Callahan says he only came once to find Josie."

Dalton stared at Chief Hayes, disbelief filtering through shock and hope. "So he admitted that was him I saw running to get into a dark car that first night when all of this started?"

"Yes." The chief got up and stared out the window. "He claims he got transferred to Utah. He's an electrician, and he has to follow the work. A new plant being built."

"And he did admit that he'd tracked Josie down?"

"Yes. Said he wanted to make amends."

"I don't believe him. I'd like to go up to Utah and question him."

"We don't have anything solid, Dalton—especially because you already showed the eyewitness a recent photo of Randall Callahan, and she couldn't be sure he was the man she saw in the parking lot. The Utah authorities have warned him not to set foot in Arizona again. He knows if we see him in Desert Valley, he will be spending time in our jail."

Dalton had to go with that for now. What else could he do?

But it was too close for comfort. And he had to tell Josie that this might finally be over, but that their main suspect wouldn't be held since they couldn't say without a doubt that he was their man. If only the eyewitness they'd interviewed could be sure. Dalton had personally gone to the woman's house and shown her the picture the Utah police had sent to him. But she couldn't verify if Randall Callahan was the man she'd seen shooting at them yesterday.

It was midafternoon by the time Dalton made it to Josie's aunt's house to pick up Maisy. Josie met him at the door, so he pulled her aside. "We need to talk."

"Okay." She took him out to the sunporch. "The kids are upstairs in the playroom. Maisy's teaching the boys how to play Monopoly."

He smiled at that. His daughter sure liked being in charge.

He sat Josie down and told her what he'd learned about Randall Callahan. "It looks like he's our man, but he didn't confess to the harassment, and he claimed he only came here once because he wanted to see you to make amends. Said his mother had gone off the deep end, and she'd blamed it all on you."

"Do you believe him?" she asked, her eyes wide with shock and distrust.

"No." Dalton wouldn't lie to her. "But his wife is vouching for him, too. Said he's been to work and back for the last few weeks, and that he did try to locate you one time but he chickened out when he saw a patrol car in your yard. Either way, the authorities in Utah have warned him to stay away from you."

"Can we be sure he'll do that?"

"According to our contact in Utah, yes. Said he kept repeating that he had a good job and a wife he loves, and he's trying to make a new life. He said he only remembered recently that you'd mentioned relatives in Arizona. He found some old letters after he cleaned out his mother's house."

"So he saw my aunt's address?"

"Yes. We think that's how he found you."

"I forgot about the couple of boxes I'd stored in her attic. It's strange that he wound up so close. Kind of makes me nervous, no matter what."

"He can't hurt you now. He told the interrogators he'd never do something like that to you. He even asked to see you."

"I'm not ready for that yet," she said. "But I do feel a sense of relief that he says it wasn't him. Do I believe him, though?"

"We have to for now. So...we go on as planned. We'll take care of the day care. Then you have the four day holiday weekend. It'll be a test to see if the threats stop. If they do, then we've scared him away."

"For now," she said. "And if it's not him?"

"We'll keep at it."

"But you still might have to leave after Christmas, Dalton."

"About that—"

Maisy burst into the room. "Daddy? When'd you get here?"

Giving Josie an apologetic smile, he said, "A few minutes ago. Ready to go home?"

Maisy nodded. "Yes. The boys won't listen to anything I say."

She hugged Josie and Marilyn, and they said their goodbyes.

"I'll call you tomorrow," Dalton said, wishing he could kiss Josie good-night.

But tomorrow could be a new start for all of them.

Monday and Tuesday morning went by without incident.

On Tuesday afternoon, Josie saw Dalton walk in the door, Luna by his side. He glanced up, searching, and found her. She smiled at him, that now-familiar warmth coursing through her system. The staff had gotten used to having K-9 officers walking around the perimeters of the property. The kids loved it, but after Josie had sent out an email explaining, a few of the parents had refused to bring their kids back. Then the local paper got wind and did an interview with her and the police chief.

Josie didn't blame anyone for their fears, but the chief had assured everyone that they had the situation under control. It was a tough call, since some of their clients didn't have anyone to watch their kids. But the place was like a fortress and the training was good for the rookies, as Dalton kept telling her.

He walked toward her now, his smile soft and sure. "So far, so good," he said. "If we get through tomorrow, I'd say we're clear."

Josie prayed toward that end. "I'm going back to my place tonight," she said. "I'll leave all the security lights on, and I have my aunt and uncle on speed dial."

"I don't like it, but I understand," Dalton said. "However, Luna and I would be willing to sleep on your couch. Or the porch."

"I don't have much of a porch, and my couch is way too small for all six feet of you."

"Too bad." He grinned and let out a sigh. "What are you doing for Christmas?"

"I'll be with my folks next door, of course," she said. Then she looked into his disappointed eyes. "Unless you and Maisy want to spend Christmas Day with me."

"I'd love that," he blurted. Then he looked sheepish. "I wasn't fishing for an invite. But I was hoping."

"Consider it a date," she replied. "Besides, my aunt will have lots of good leftovers."

"The best of both worlds," he replied in a whisper. "I'll have you to myself for a while, and then I'll have leftovers later."

She grinned at that and waved as he and Maisy left. Whitney and Zoe escorted Josie, her aunt and the rest of the staff to their cars.

Josie spent the evening wrapping gifts. She'd managed to pick up a few things when Zoe invited her to go shopping yesterday after work. She'd bought Maisy a scarf, and she'd found a nice pair of gloves for Dalton.

She'd pulled back the covers to go to bed when her cell rang. Her heart filled with dread; Josie didn't recognize the number.

Answering with trepidation, she held her breath.

"The Desert Valley Day care is on fire."

TWELVE

Dalton pulled to the curb, tires screeching as he jumped out of the patrol car. "Maisy, stay with Luna."

His blurry-eyed daughter nodded. "Daddy, don't let it burn down."

"Stay there," he told her. Poor kid was still in her pajamas underneath her puffy coat, but he had to come and he couldn't leave her at home.

When he saw Josie standing with Marilyn and Jack, he hurried over to her. "Josie?"

She turned and fell into his arms, her eyes full of tears. "He tried to burn it down, Dalton."

"I'm so sorry," Dalton said, holding her close. "I thought we had our man but I don't see how Randall would try this knowing we're on to him."

"It had to be Randall," she said, pulling away, her eyes full of anger.

Dalton couldn't comfort her. He'd failed her, and it was evident from the look on her face that she thought that, too.

Zoe hurried up. "I just heard. Do you think it was Callahan?"

"We need to find out," Dalton said. "Call the local police station in Utah." He gave her the number. "Thanks, Zoe."

Zoe hurried off, her phone in her hand.

Chief Hayes rushed toward them from the back of the building. "Started near the fuse box. Electrical."

"Electrical?" Josie tugged at her coat. "Randall's an electrician. What more proof do we need?"

"Unfortunately, a lot more," Chief Hayes said.

Dalton felt as helpless as Josie. "Officer Trent is notifying the authorities in Utah, sir. We should hear soon if Callahan is involved. Meantime, we can put out a BOLO."

Dalton watched as tired firemen walked by and went about cleaning up and putting away their equipment. The fire chief came up to Josie and Marilyn. "We managed to put it out, but the kitchen and back part of the building aren't safe. You'll need to shut it down for repairs."

Josie nodded, her fingers pressed to her lips. When Dalton reached for her, she pushed away and headed to the back of the building. "I want to see how bad it looks."

"I'll go check on her," Marilyn said. "Jack, go see about the boys. They might have driven our SUV away by now."

Her husband hurried to where their big vehicle was parked, but one of the firemen stopped Marilyn to ask her a question. That left Dalton standing alone, the smell of burned wires and scorched wood stifling him. When he heard Luna's agitated bark, he whirled.

And saw the door to the patrol car standing open.

Maisy wasn't there.

Josie heard a dog barking in the front parking lot. Wiping at her tears, she turned from the rubble that had once been the storage room and the day care kitchen.

Now she would lose her clients because of fear and not having a place to leave their children. Her life here was over. And for what? Some sort of revenge quest?

When she heard the barking again, she turned and saw a purple backpack lying near the fence. And then she noticed the back gate to the day care property standing open.

With a gasp, she rushed toward the backpack and grabbed it up.

Maisy!

Josie gulped in a breath and turned to find Dalton running toward her, panic on his face. Luna whizzed past him and into the woods, turning to bark before she danced around toward the dark brambles.

Dalton took one look at the backpack and shook his head. "No. No." Then he called out to Luna. "Find. Find Maisy."

Luna barked and lunged forward.

Dalton took off running after her.

Maisy was gone.

Josie held to the backpack and followed him into the woods. She could hear him shouting for help. Luna's barking sounded off in the distance.

Please, Lord, let them find Maisy safe and sound.

But before she could catch up with Dalton, someone grabbed her from behind and clamped a grimy hand over her mouth. Dropping the backpack, Josie struggled, but that only made the man tighten his grip.

"You're coming with me," he said. "We end this tonight."

"Maisy?"

Dalton was hoarse from calling her name. Luna stayed up ahead, racing through the woods until they came out on the other side of the road.

And into the yard with the abandoned car and old, deserted house.

Dalton swallowed the excruciating pain coursing through him. The pain of failure, the pain of knowing he'd been close to the truth the last time he'd been here and he'd found nothing.

Nothing. But now, his daughter might be in there, hurt. Or worse.

Dear God…

He couldn't finish the words. He hoped God would hear his plea. Luna stopped at the side door of the house. Now she emitted low growls. Her way of warning Dalton while she alerted.

Someone was in there.

Dalton pulled his weapon and prayed Zoe and the chief would follow the trail. His phone buzzed, and he quickly checked the message.

It was Randall Callahan. Josie's brother-in-law remembered someone inquiring about Josie. A coworker of her husband's named Wilson or possibly Wilcox?

Dalton put away his phone, his gut burning. They'd been targeting the wrong man.

Josie. He remembered her holding the backpack, her eyes wide with fear and horror. She'd want to help find Maisy. She loved his daughter, too.

Blinking back his emotions, Dalton slowly made his way to the old, battered door and stared into the window. A flashlight lay on the floor, illuminating enough of the room for him to see Maisy sitting in a chair, her arms tied behind her so she couldn't escape. A slow rage boiled up inside Dalton. He was about to kick down the door when he heard a sound behind him. Dalton turned and found a dirty, scruffy-looking man holding Josie, his arm stretched across her neck.

And a gun jammed against her side.

Josie shouted, "Dalton, get down."

The man shot and missed. She cried out, but he held the gun to her head. "I'll kill her," he shouted to Dalton. "Put down the gun and hold that dog back."

Luna's growls turned to aggressive barks.

Dalton halted her. "Stay." He held his gun out and slowly lowered it to the ground.

When Josie heard cries of "Daddy" from inside the house, she breathed a sigh of relief. Maisy was alive.

"I'm coming," Dalton called. "Maisy, honey, stay right where you are. Don't try to untie your hands. Stay there, baby."

"She can't get away," the man said. "Y'all are gonna have to join her. And then it'll finally be over."

Josie gave Dalton a warning glance. "He's not my brother-in-law. He's—"

"Perry Wilcox," Dalton guessed. "The one missing link that we couldn't find." He nodded toward the man. "You worked with Josie's husband, right?"

The man shoved Josie toward the house. "That's right. I finally found her. This woman ruined my life, so I tried to ruin hers."

"By threatening her with strange notes and letters and shooting at her?" Dalton asked. "And now, kidnapping a child, too?"

"I had to get everyone's attention," the man shouted. "No one ever listens to me."

Dalton kept his eyes on Josie. She stared at him, trying to convey all that she felt at this moment—gratitude, fear for him and Maisy, hope and dread, and love. A love so strong that she knew she had to survive this, somehow.

"He thinks I caused the accident at the refinery," she said, trying to keep her voice steady. "Douglas and I had a horrible fight that day before his shift. Mr. Wilcox cleaned up hazardous spills and…something went wrong."

The man pushed her closer to Dalton. Luna growled low in her throat, her impatience evident in her body language.

"I'll show you what went wrong." Wilcox turned, and Josie felt sick to her stomach. He had a horrid scar on the left side of his face. His skin had been scorched and burned. "This! My marriage ended, and I lost my job." He jerked his arm tighter around Josie. "The accident was Douglas Callahan's fault. In the weeks before it, he always came to work drunk. He told us how horrible Josie was, how she didn't want a family or children. How lazy she was. Not a good wife. He was so mad at her, he couldn't focus and he messed up big-time."

Dalton's eyes held Josie's, an understanding passing between them. "So her actions ruined your life and you had to make her pay, right?"

Wilcox bobbed his head. "Right. I tried to shut down that kiddie corral. And I'm not done."

Dalton inched closer. "You don't have to do this. We can help you. I'll make sure she gets what she deserves." Josie knew Dalton was bargaining, anything, to make the man think he was on his side.

Wilcox shook his head. "I don't care anymore. I can't let her live when my life is over." He pressed the gun into Josie's ribs. "Get inside. I want her to tell me how sorry she is. I want her to beg."

Josie tried to keep breathing. She could get out of this. She had to help Maisy and Dalton. She wouldn't let them die because of this madman and his misguided sense of justice.

"Just take *me*," she said. "Let them go and take me with you. I'll do whatever you want if you let them go."

"Ain't gonna work," he said. "Now let's get inside."

Before the man could force them into the house, they heard a shuffling noise and a door slamming. Startled, Wilcox looked to the left.

It was all the distraction Josie and Dalton needed. Josie elbowed him in the ribs, stomped on his foot and then shoved him back. She dove to the ground a few feet out of his reach. Dalton grabbed his gun and rushed the man. Luna started barking again.

"Attack," Dalton called, rolling away so Luna could do her job.

Maisy came running around the building, holding a large tree branch. When Josie saw the girl, she grabbed her and held her back. "It's okay, Maisy. I'm okay. We're all okay."

Maisy dropped the big limb and turned and fell into Josie's arms, her sobs echoing out over the stark woods. "I kept working at the ropes until I could slip through them."

"You did great, honey."

When they heard more barking, Dalton called off Luna and cuffed Perry Wilcox. "Don't move!"

Then he turned and hurried to his daughter and Josie. "It's over," he said. "It's all over."

Christmas Day

Josie stood in her kitchen and smiled at the man sitting with his daughter on the couch. Dalton and Maisy had opened their presents at home, and now they'd come to spend Christmas with her. Dalton was admiring his gloves, and Maisy was wrapping her scarf in much the same way she'd seen Josie wearing hers.

Josie thanked God for this scene. When Dalton got up to refresh his coffee and grab another cinnamon roll, she couldn't help it. She hugged him close. "Thank you for the hand lotion."

He sniffed her hair. "You always smell so good, it reminded me of you."

"It's so good to be alive," she said. "We're so blessed."

He nuzzled her ear. "Yes."

The horror of her encounter with Perry Wilcox still held her, though. "I'm just glad it's over."

They had Wilcox in custody. The eyewitness had identified him as the man she'd seen in the town center parking lot, and the can of red spray paint left behind was what was used on her fence and her car. The lab had actually found a partial print on the can that was a match.

"We're here, together, and it's cold, but we're warm and safe," Dalton said. "I'm cleared to start my assignment next week in Canyon County instead of Flagstaff. I won't have to leave you."

They glanced at Maisy and Luna, curled up together. Maisy was now reading a book she'd received from Santa, and Luna enjoyed a chew bone from her doggie stocking.

"We have a big day," Josie said. "Zoe, Sean and Patrick are coming over for dinner and bringing Freya, and then we'll go over to my aunt's for even more food."

"I love it," Dalton said. "And I love you."

Josie's heart dipped and lifted. "I thought we were going to take this slow."

"We will," he said. "But I can love you while we do that."

"I love you, too," she admitted. "I love Maisy and I owe Luna my life."

"I'll remind you of that every day for the next fifty years."

She smiled at him, and then he dipped his head to give her a quick but thorough kiss. "Let's hurry up and take this slow."

When the doorbell rang, Maisy jumped up. "May I get it?"

Dalton laughed. "Make sure you know who it is first."

He'd had a talk with his brave daughter. She'd untied her hands in spite of his warnings. Or because of his warnings, since he'd tried to teach her how to survive in any situation. Maisy was bold, but he wanted her to be cautious, too.

Dalton gave Josie another kiss before the house filled with laughter and joy. Freya greeted her friend Luna with a doggie woof and then settled down beside Luna to enjoy the day.

Maisy took Patrick by the hand. "Wanna see what I got for Christmas?"

The little boy grinned and showed her his gift, his speech still slow and stilted but improving. "I got a game."

Zoe hugged Josie and gave her a reassuring smile, while Dalton offered Sean a drink. "You sure look happy."

"I am," Josie replied. "I can't believe the police department volunteered to throw us a party and help us rebuild the day care."

Sean grinned and held up his drink. "And we're keeping our children with you. We trust you, Josie."

Josie found it hard to speak. "I can't wait to get back to work."

"Well, meantime, your aunt has the situation under control," Zoe said. "She was licensed to care for children in her home for years, and she's still good to go."

After they gathered around the dining table, Josie took Dalton's hand. "Will you say grace?"

Dalton looked sheepish. "Yes, I'll be glad to. I have the best Christmas gift. My family."

When he finished, Maisy screamed and ran to the window. "Daddy, look. It's snowing!"

Josie couldn't believe it. Beautiful, delicate snowflakes fell like lace and covered the ground.

Maisy grabbed Patrick. "This is a perfect Christmas."

Josie looked around the table and then met Dalton's gaze. Maisy was right. After so much pain, they were able to celebrate the gift of Christ together. She was home.

* * * * *

If you enjoyed
ROOKIE K-9 UNIT CHRISTMAS,
look for the rest of the
ROOKIE K-9 UNIT series:

PROTECT AND SERVE
by Terri Reed

TRUTH AND CONSEQUENCES
by Lenora Worth

SEEK AND FIND
by Dana Mentink

HONOR AND DEFEND
by Lynette Eason

SECRETS AND LIES
by Shirlee McCoy

SEARCH AND RESCUE
by Valerie Hansen

Dear Reader,

I enjoyed being part of this novella collection with my friend Valerie Hansen. It was good to revisit Desert Valley, Arizona, and see what was happening with some of the K-9 Unit characters a few months later.

My heart went out to Josie and Dalton. Josie wanted a family but she'd almost given up. Dalton once had a family, but the loss of his wife devastated him and his little girl. Maisy wanted to protect everyone because she thought she had failed at protecting her mother. I think we all have felt this way at times. We wish we could protect everyone we love and keep them from pain. I hope that if you've had a sad event in your life, this book might help you to see that God's love covers all hurts, and our faith can help us to heal. The K-9 dog in this book is named after my granddog, Luna. Luna is protective of those she loves and we all love her, too.

Until next time, may the angels watch over you. Always. :)

Lenora Worth